S0-DXD-807

GEAR HERO

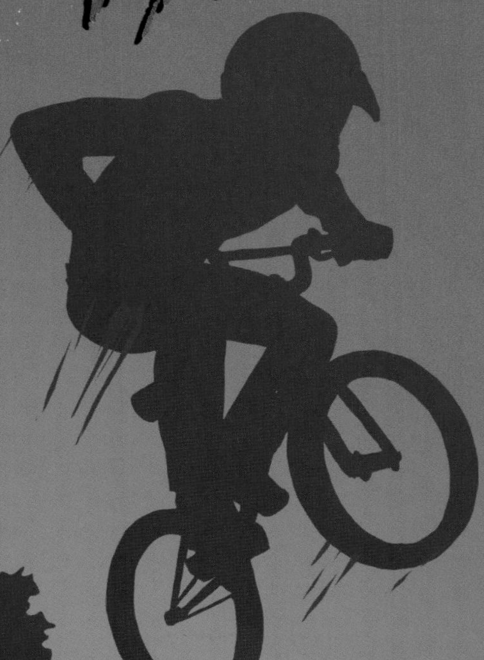

STONE ARCH BOOKS
a capstone imprint

JAKE MADDOX
GRAPHIC NOVELS

Jake Maddox Graphic Novels are published by
Stone Arch Books, a Capstone imprint
1710 Roe Crest Drive
North Mankato, Minnesota 56003

www.mycapstone.com

Copyright © 2019 Stone Arch Books

All rights reserved. No part of this publication may
be reproduced in whole or in part, or stored in a
retrieval system, or transmitted in any form or by
any means, electronic, mechanical, photocopying,
recording, or otherwise, without written permission
of the publisher.

Library of Congress Cataloging-in-Publication Data
is available on the Library of Congress website at
https://lccn.loc.gov/2018005697

ISBN: 978-1-4965-6045-2 (library binding)
ISBN: 978-1-4965-6049-0 (paperback)
ISBN: 978-1-4965-6053-7 (ebook PDF)

Summary: Nelson Greenwood loves drawing
superheroes, particularly Major Speed—the hero of
his own comic book. Nelson modeled Major Speed
after his twin brother Nick, a skilled BMX rider.
However, when a crash knocks Nick out of a big
race, he suggests that Nelson take his place. But
Nelson isn't sure he can summon the courage and
skill of Major Speed to compete against the best
BMX riders, especially Nick's biggest nemesis—
Cain Otto.

Editor: Aaron Sautter
Designer: Brann Garvey
Production: Tori Abraham

Printed in the United States of America.
PA021

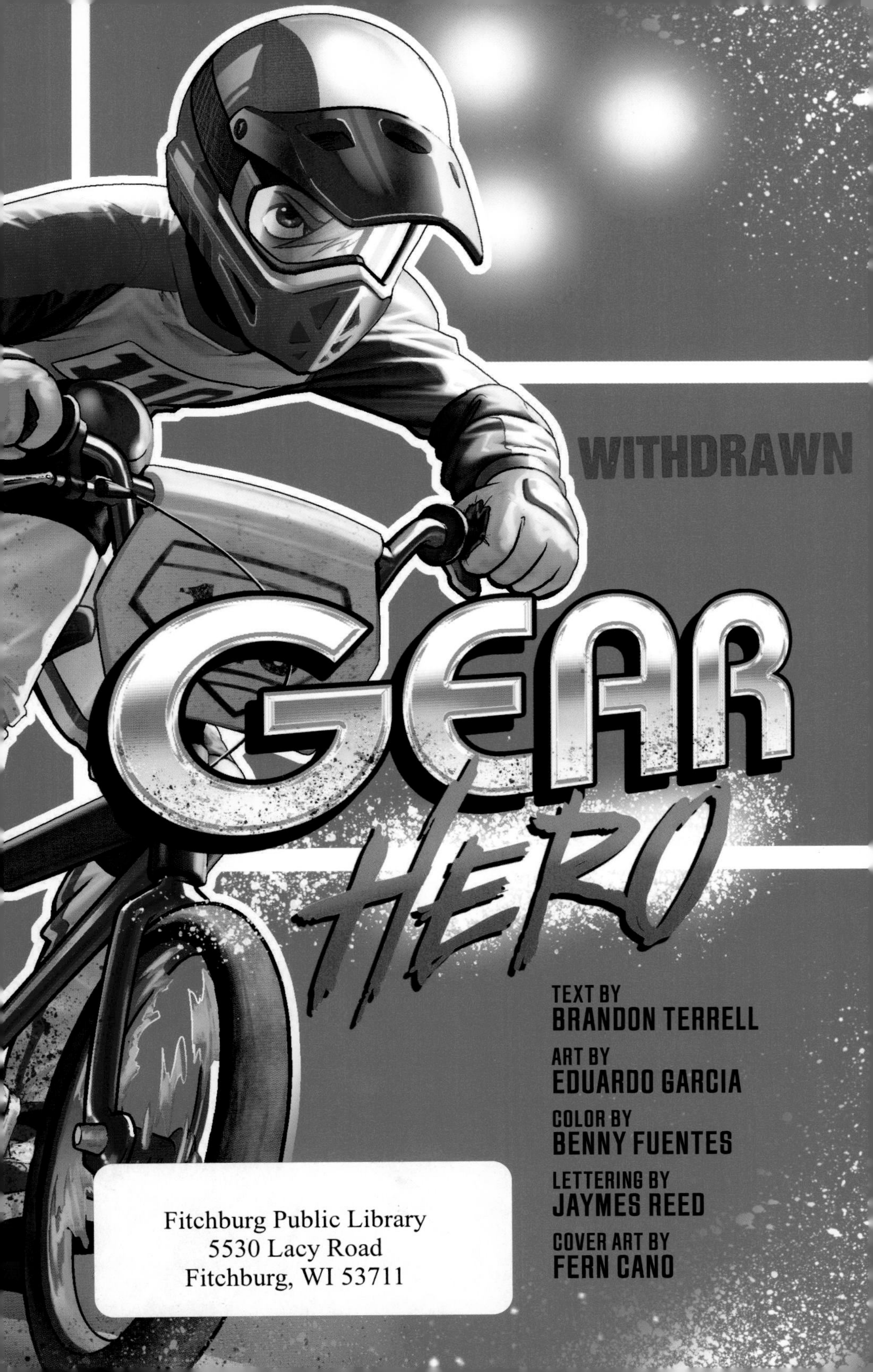

GEAR HERO

TEXT BY
BRANDON TERRELL

ART BY
EDUARDO GARCIA

COLOR BY
BENNY FUENTES

LETTERING BY
JAYMES REED

COVER ART BY
FERN CANO

CAST OF CHARACTERS

NELSON GREENWOOD

NICK GREENWOOD

CAIN OTTO

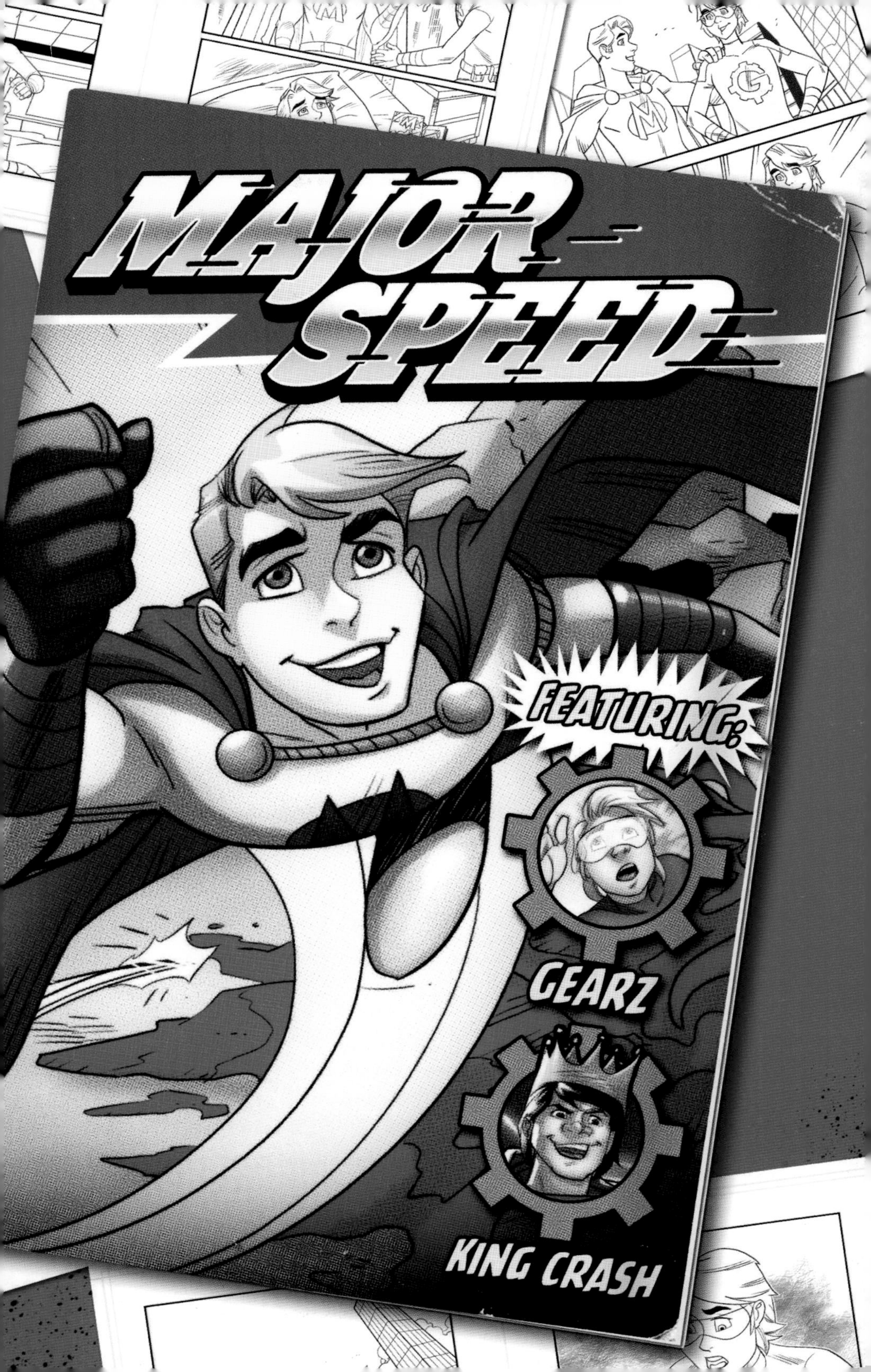
MAJOR SPEED
FEATURING:
GEARZ
KING CRASH

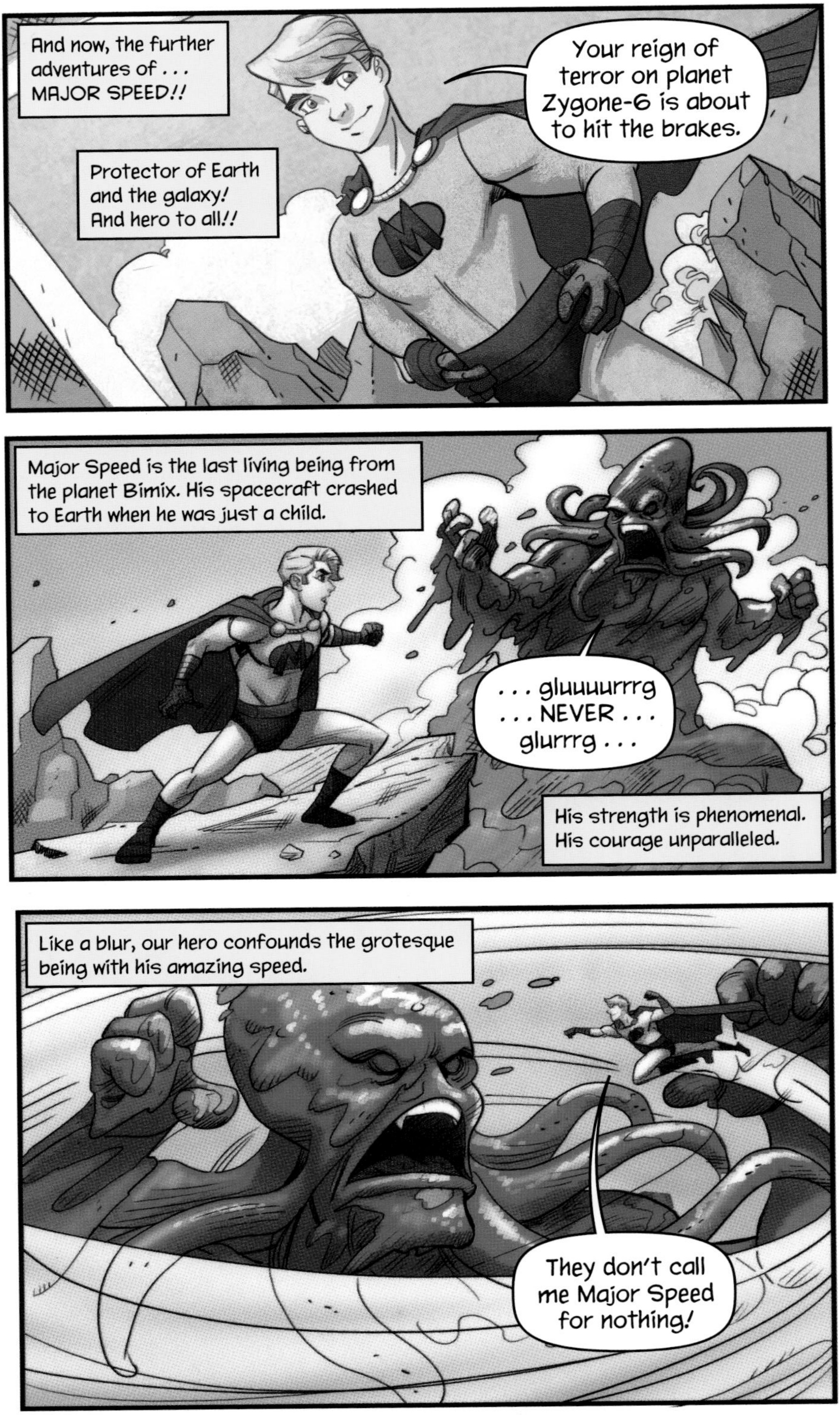
And now, the further adventures of . . . MAJOR SPEED!!
Your reign of terror on planet Zygone-6 is about to hit the brakes.
Protector of Earth and the galaxy! And hero to all!!
Major Speed is the last living being from the planet Bimix. His spacecraft crashed to Earth when he was just a child.
. . . gluuuurrrg . . . NEVER . . . glurrrg . . .
His strength is phenomenal. His courage unparalleled.
Like a blur, our hero confounds the grotesque being with his amazing speed.
They don't call me Major Speed for nothing!

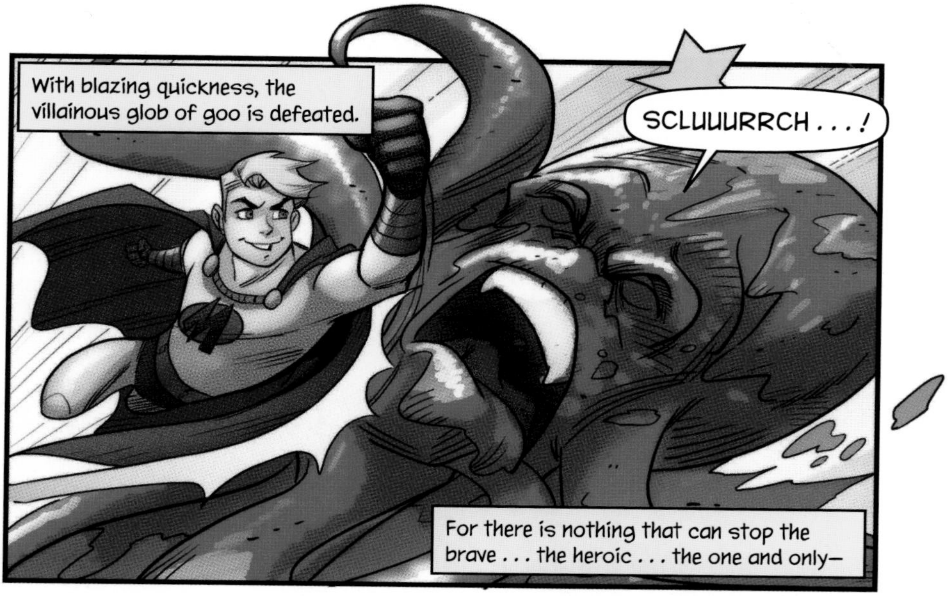
With blazing quickness, the villainous glob of goo is defeated.
SCLUUURRCH . . . !
For there is nothing that can stop the brave . . . the heroic . . . the one and only—

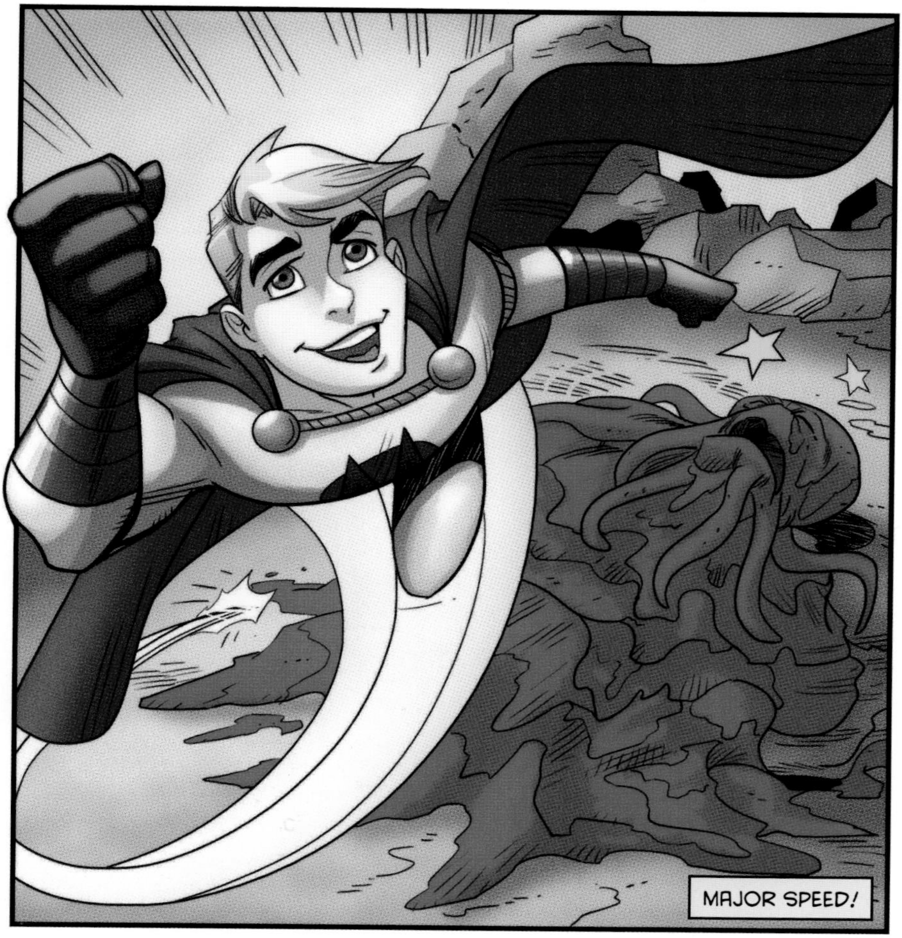
MAJOR SPEED!

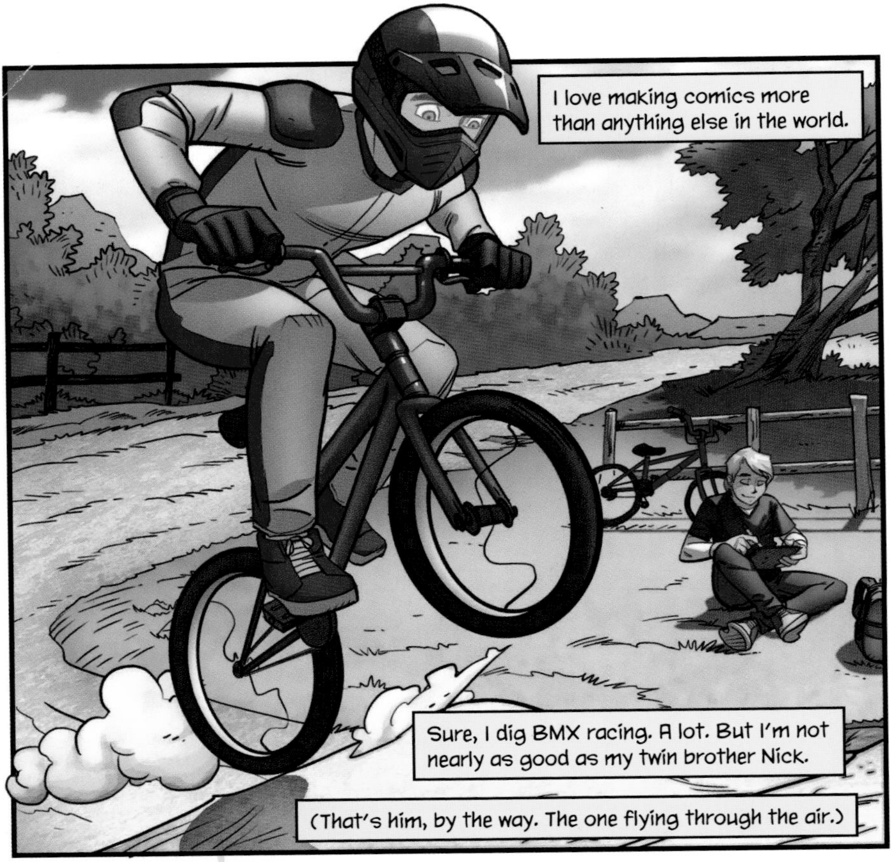
I love making comics more than anything else in the world.
Sure, I dig BMX racing. A lot. But I'm not nearly as good as my twin brother Nick.
(That's him, by the way. The one flying through the air.)

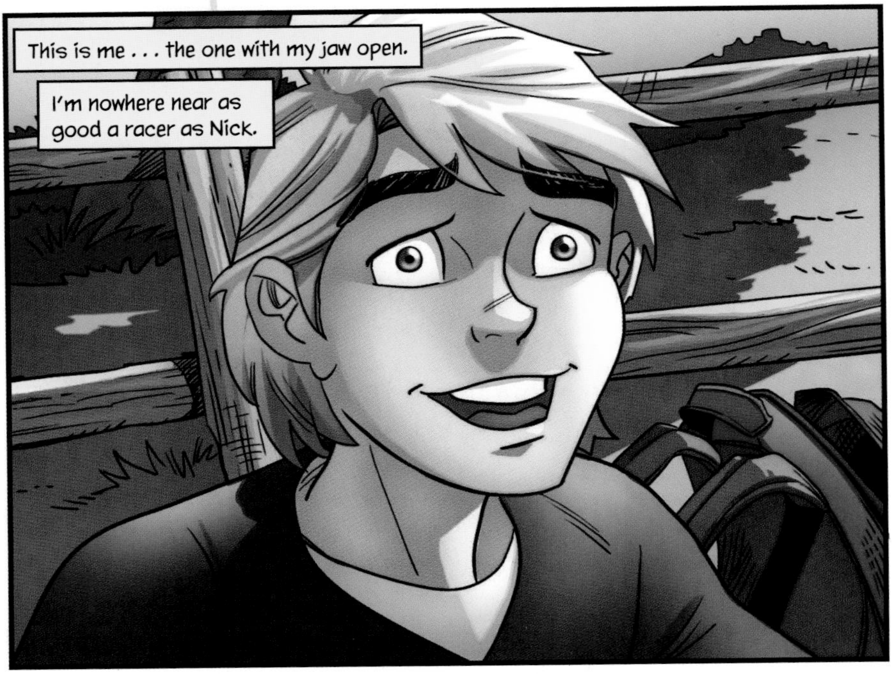
This is me . . . the one with my jaw open.
I'm nowhere near as good a racer as Nick.

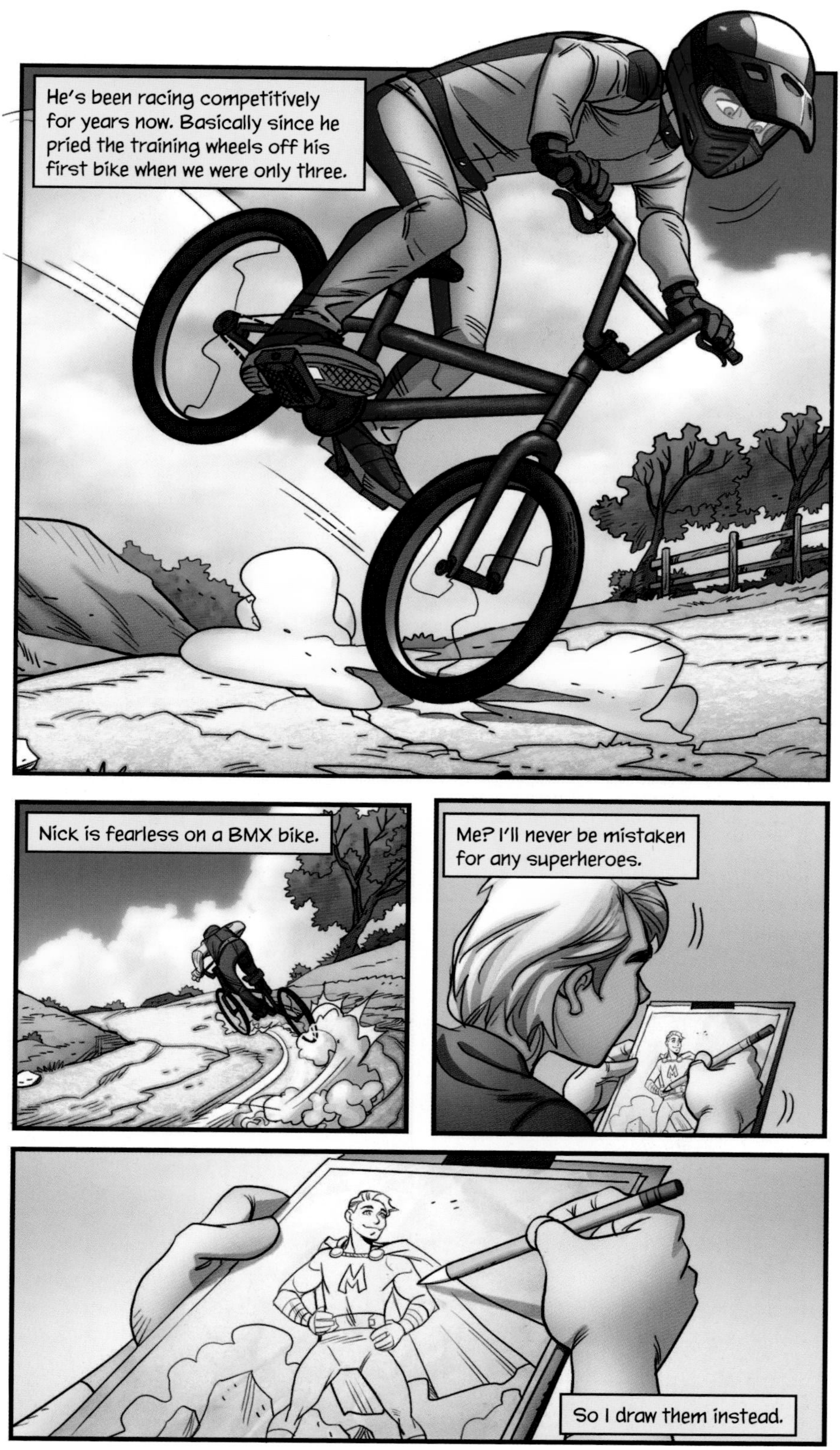
He's been racing competitively for years now. Basically since he pried the training wheels off his first bike when we were only three.
Nick is fearless on a BMX bike.
Me? I'll never be mistaken for any superheroes.
So I draw them instead.

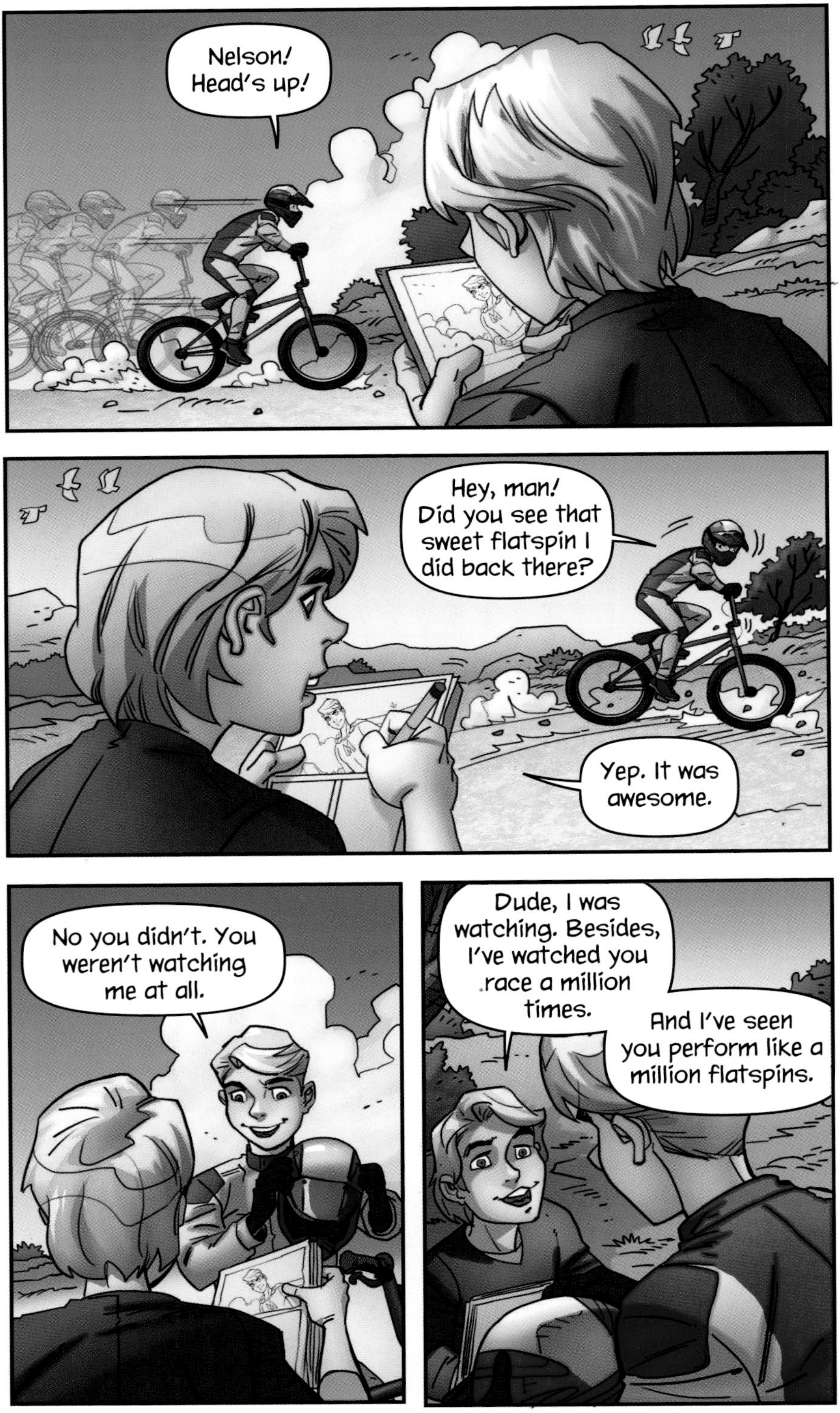

Nelson! Head's up!
Hey, man! Did you see that sweet flatspin I did back there?
Yep. It was awesome.
No you didn't. You weren't watching me at all.
Dude, I was watching. Besides, I've watched you race a million times.
And I've seen you perform like a million flatspins.

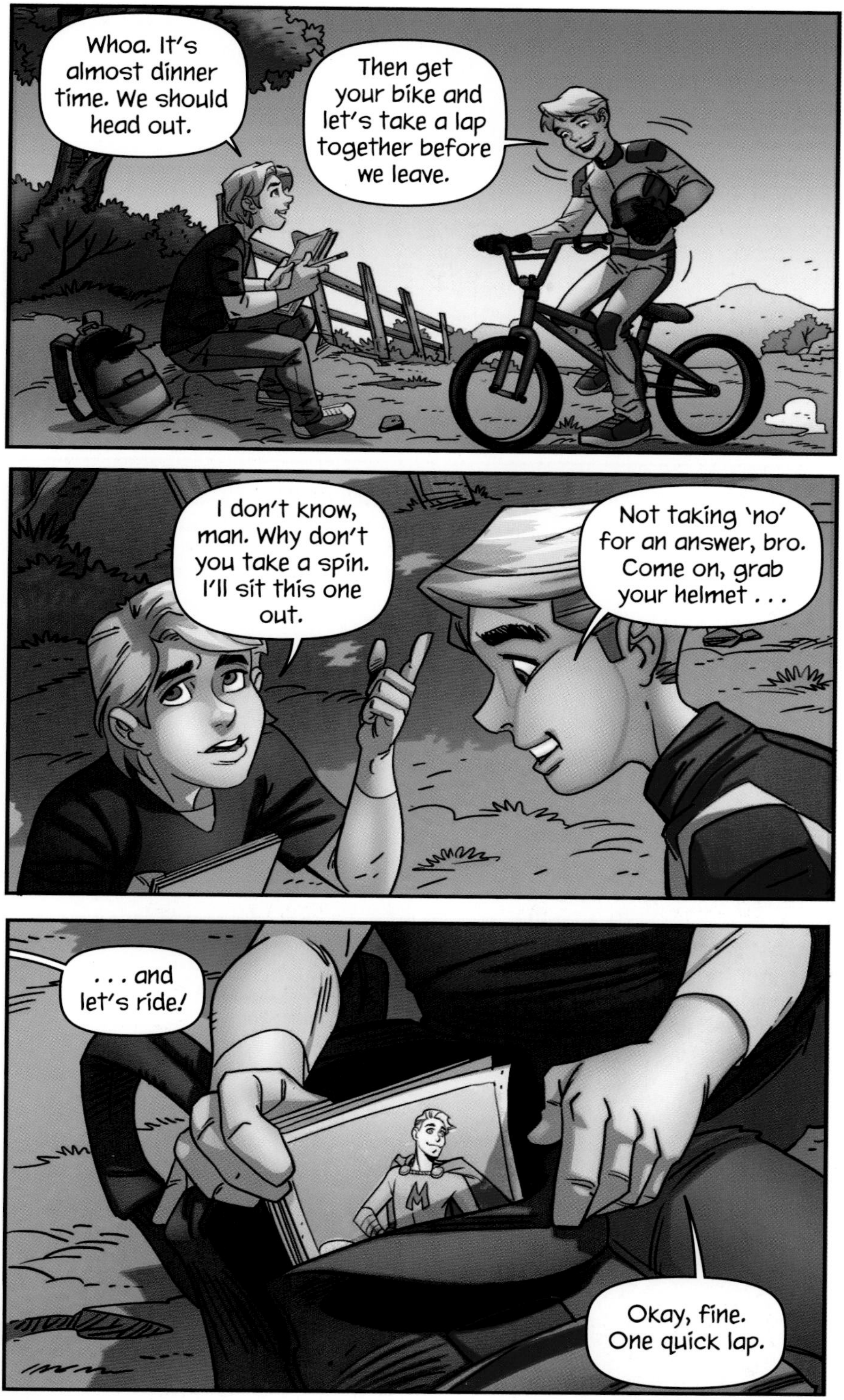
Whoa. It's almost dinner time. We should head out.
Then get your bike and let's take a lap together before we leave.
I don't know, man. Why don't you take a spin. I'll sit this one out.
Not taking 'no' for an answer, bro. Come on, grab your helmet . . .
. . . and let's ride!
Okay, fine. One quick lap.

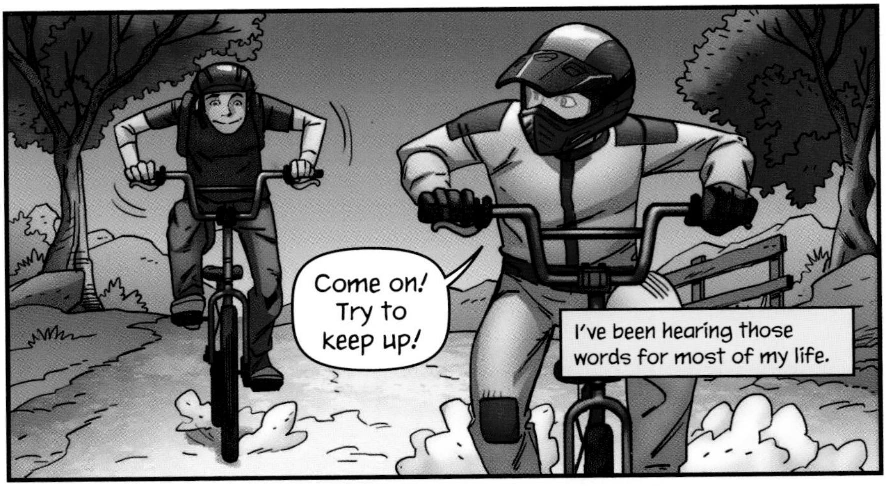
Come on! Try to keep up!
I've been hearing those words for most of my life.

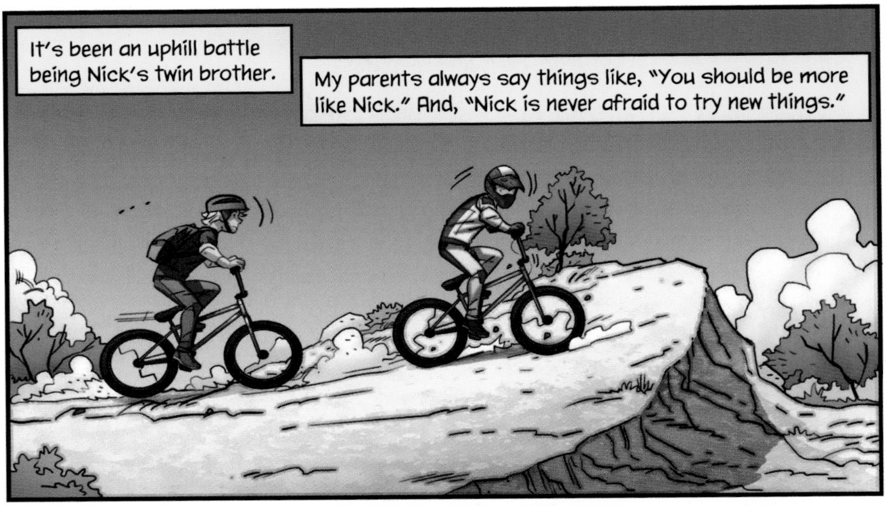
It's been an uphill battle being Nick's twin brother.
My parents always say things like, "You should be more like Nick." And, "Nick is never afraid to try new things."

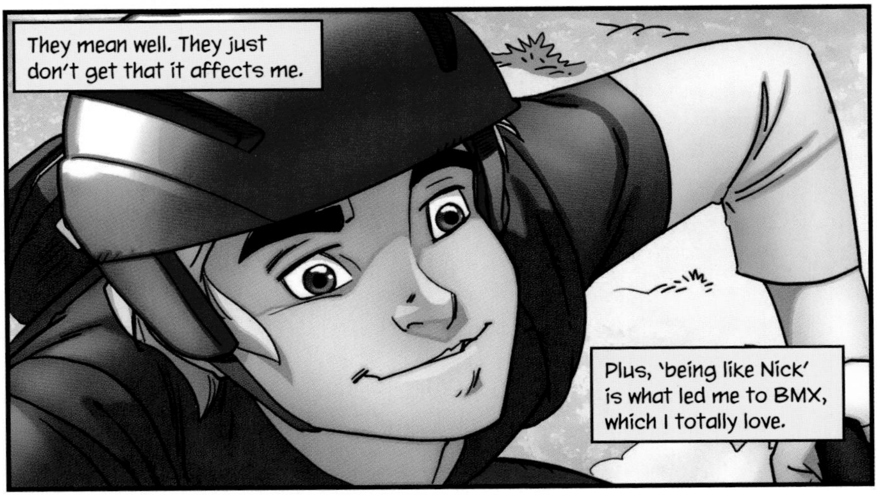
They mean well. They just don't get that it affects me.
Plus, 'being like Nick' is what led me to BMX, which I totally love.

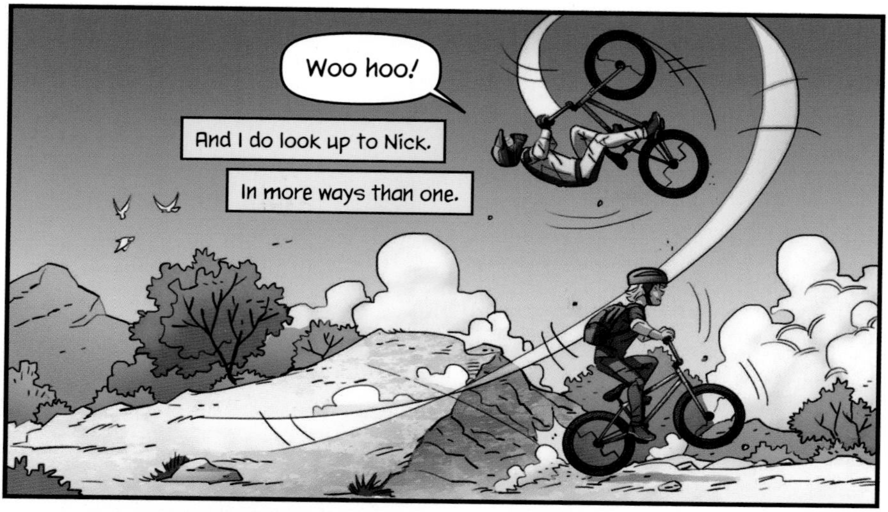
Woo hoo!
And I do look up to Nick.
In more ways than one.

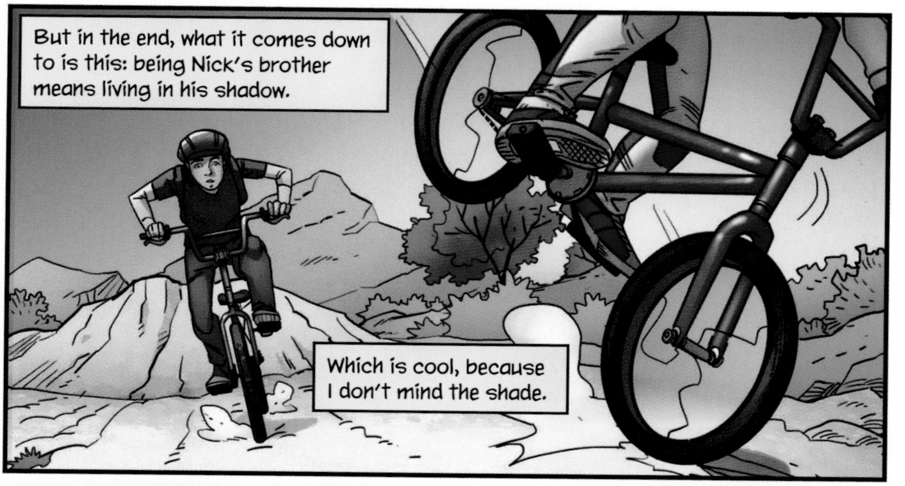
But in the end, what it comes down to is this: being Nick's brother means living in his shadow.
Which is cool, because I don't mind the shade.

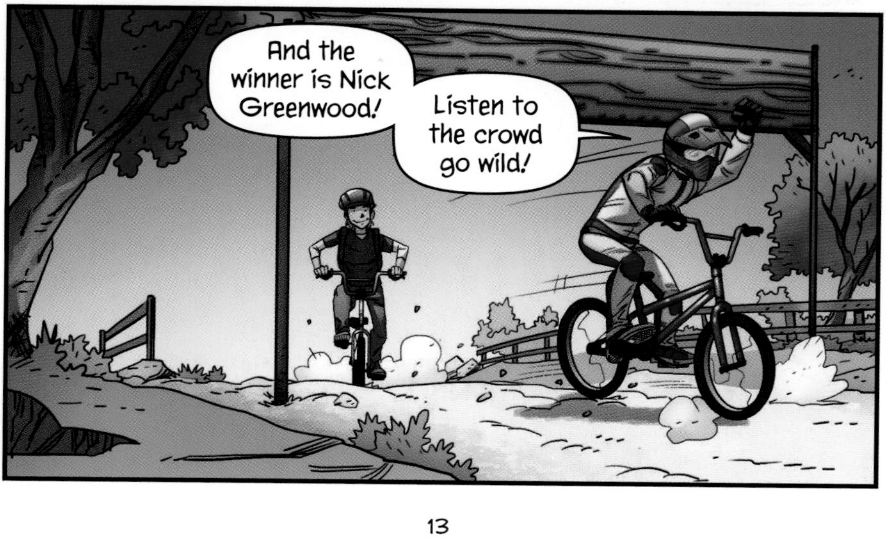
And the winner is Nick Greenwood!
Listen to the crowd go wild!

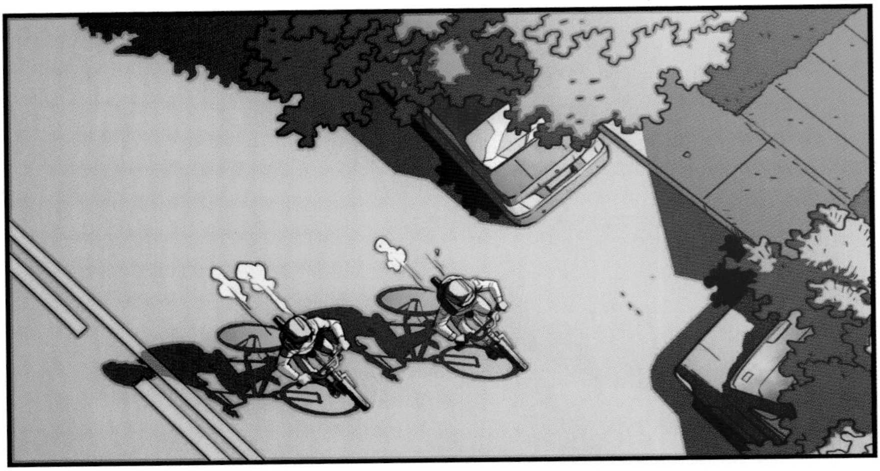

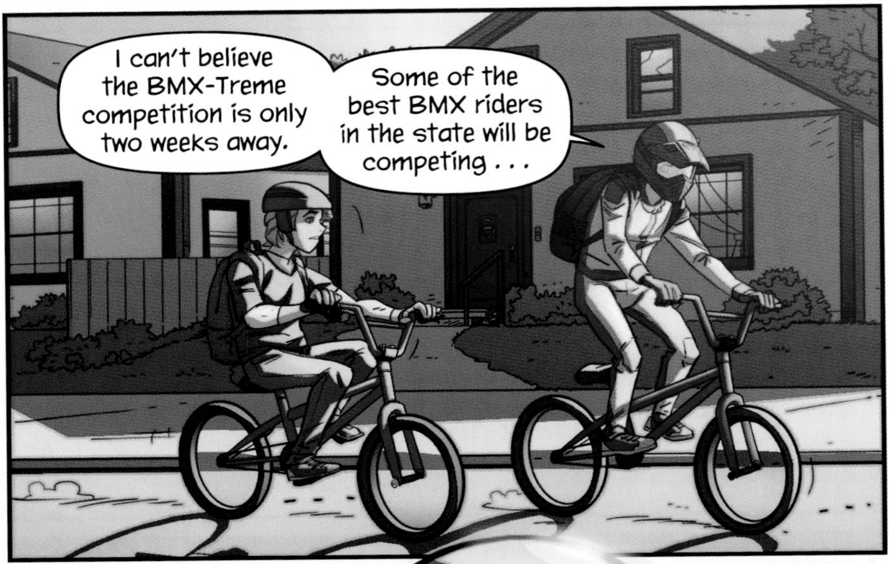
I can't believe the BMX-Treme competition is only two weeks away.
Some of the best BMX riders in the state will be competing . . .

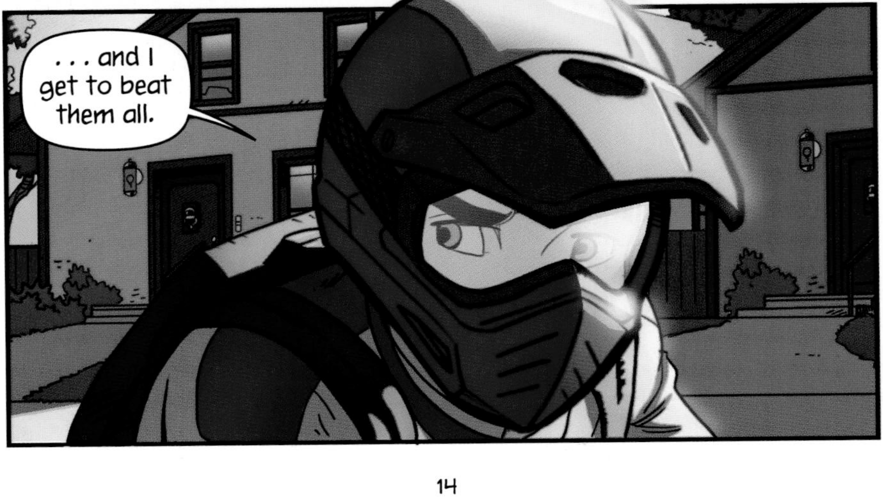
. . . and I get to beat them all.

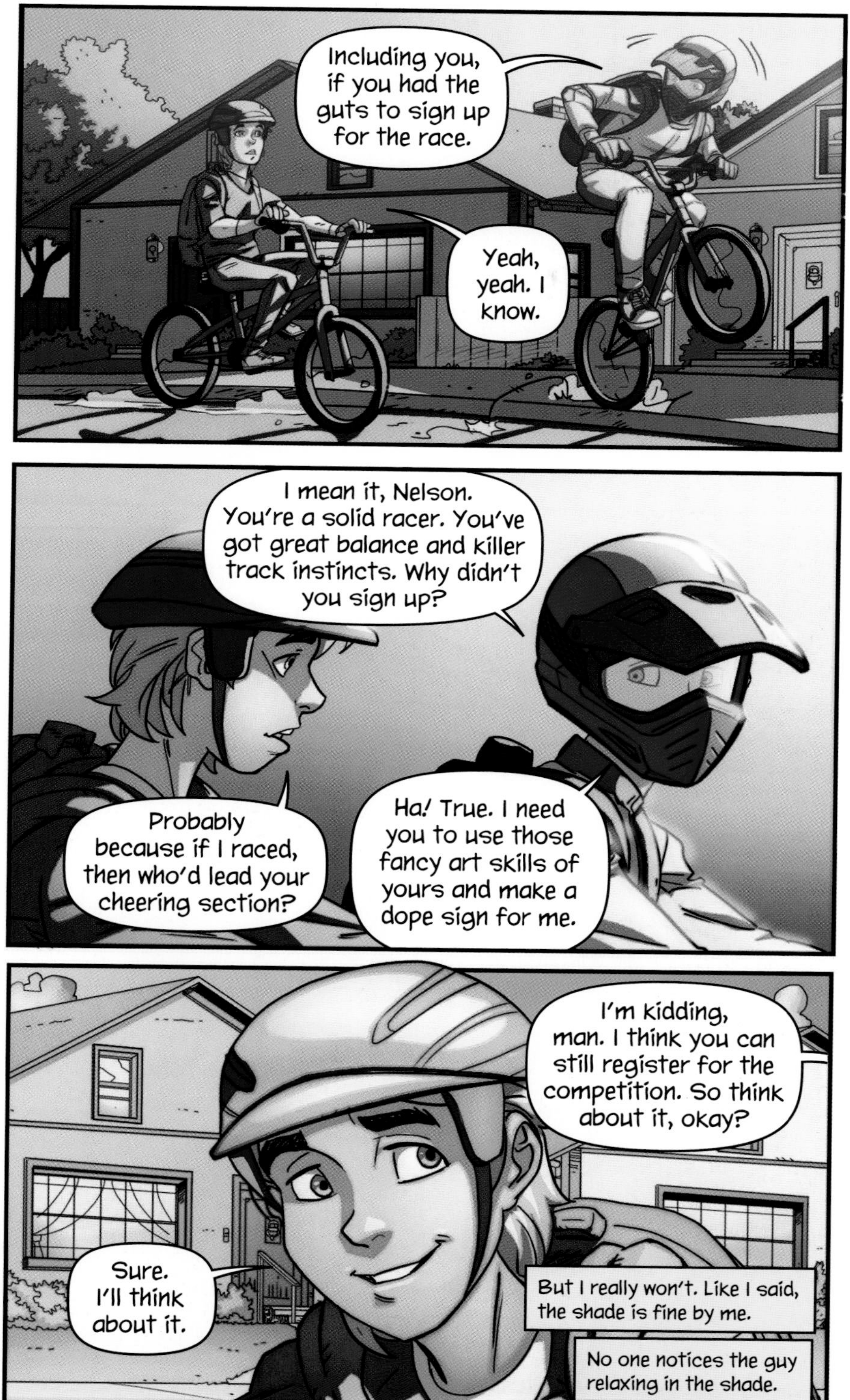

Including you, if you had the guts to sign up for the race.
Yeah, yeah. I know.
I mean it, Nelson. You're a solid racer. You've got great balance and killer track instincts. Why didn't you sign up?
Probably because if I raced, then who'd lead your cheering section?
Ha! True. I need you to use those fancy art skills of yours and make a dope sign for me.
I'm kidding, man. I think you can still register for the competition. So think about it, okay?
Sure. I'll think about it.
But I really won't. Like I said, the shade is fine by me.
No one notices the guy relaxing in the shade.

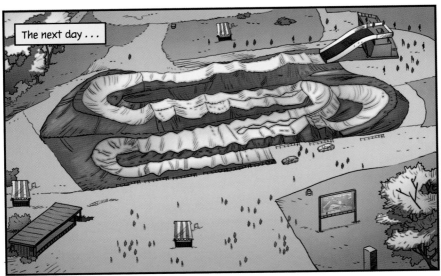

The next day . . .

Whoa, this place is crazy busy. Wanna take a practice lap with me?

Nah. I'm gonna hit the concession stands and find a place to sit. Maybe I'll start making a sign that says Nick Greenwood's #1 Fan. What color should I use? I'm thinking all of them.

Come on, man. Let's at least check out the track conditions.

You don't need me, bro. Remember? You're unstoppable.

Ha! Unstoppable? I doubt it.

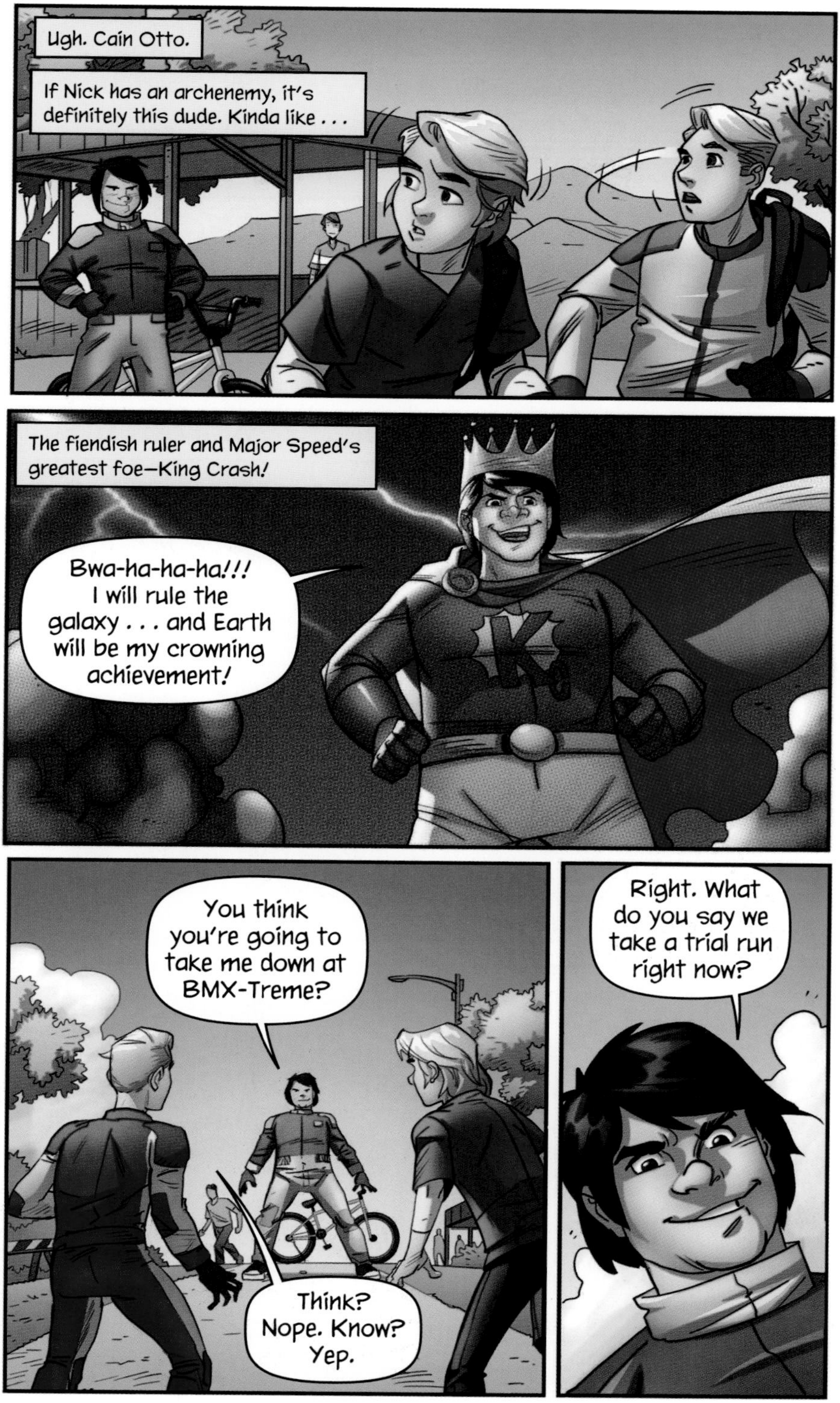
Ugh. Cain Otto.
If Nick has an archenemy, it's definitely this dude. Kinda like . . .
The fiendish ruler and Major Speed's greatest foe—King Crash!
Bwa-ha-ha-ha!!! I will rule the galaxy . . . and Earth will be my crowning achievement!
You think you're going to take me down at BMX-Treme?
Think? Nope. Know? Yep.
Right. What do you say we take a trial run right now?

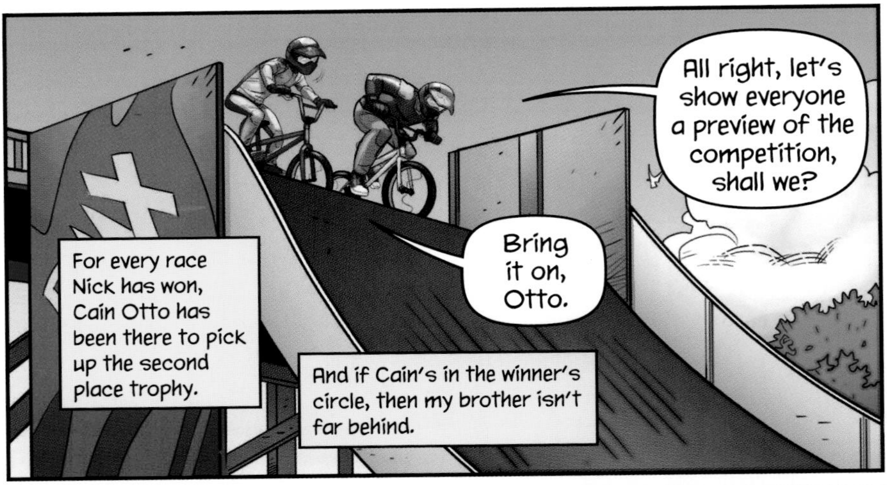
All right, let's show everyone a preview of the competition, shall we?
Bring it on, Otto.
For every race Nick has won, Cain Otto has been there to pick up the second place trophy.
And if Cain's in the winner's circle, then my brother isn't far behind.

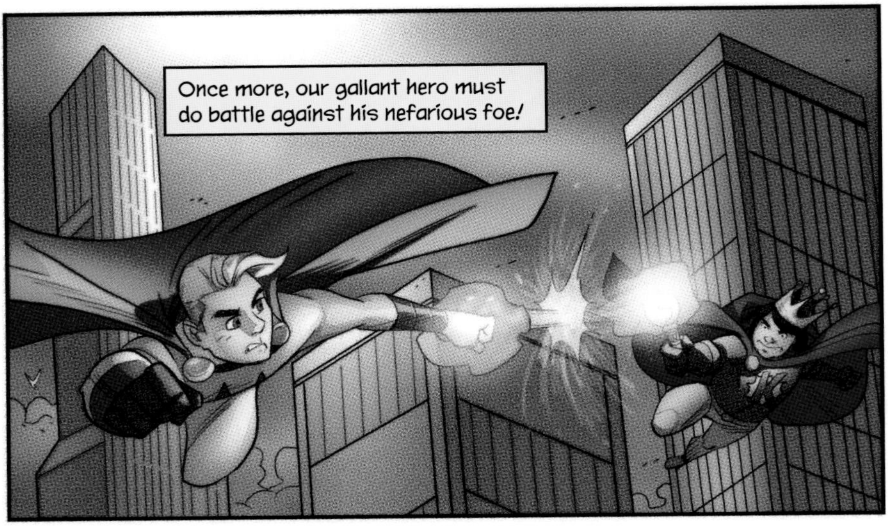
Once more, our gallant hero must do battle against his nefarious foe!

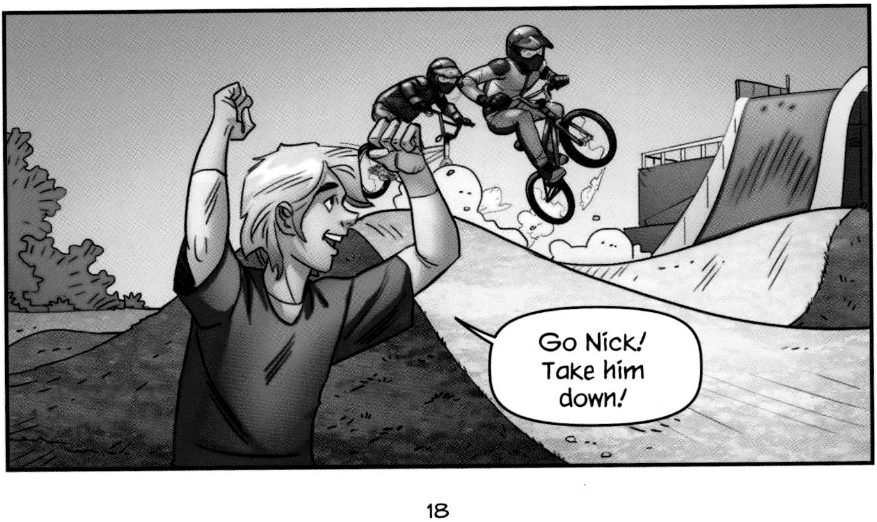
Go Nick! Take him down!

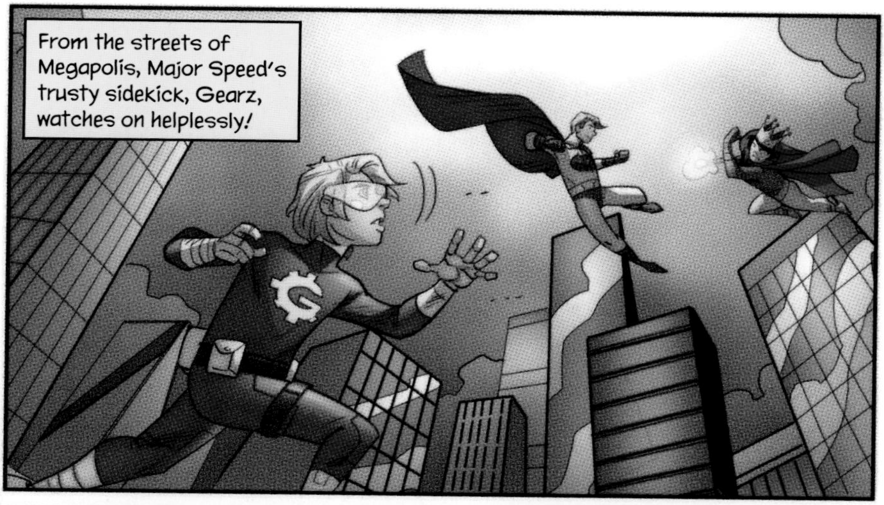
From the streets of Megapolis, Major Speed's trusty sidekick, Gearz, watches on helplessly!

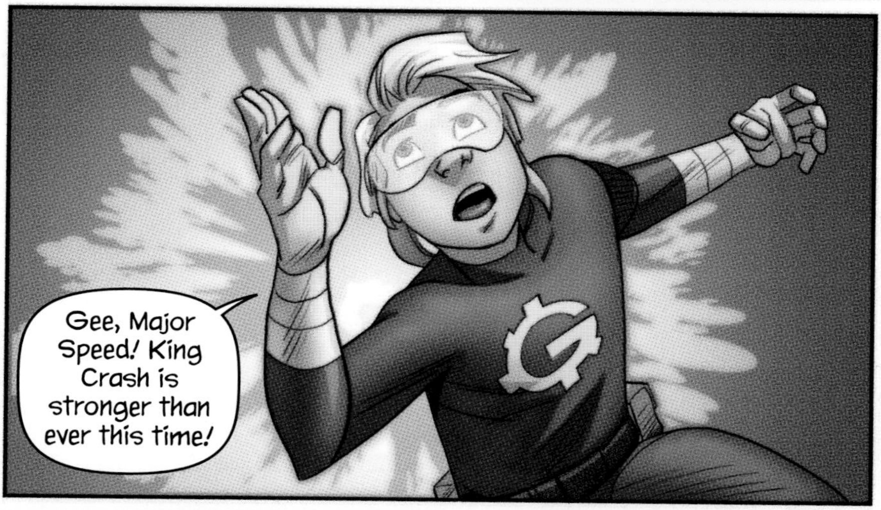
Gee, Major Speed! King Crash is stronger than ever this time!

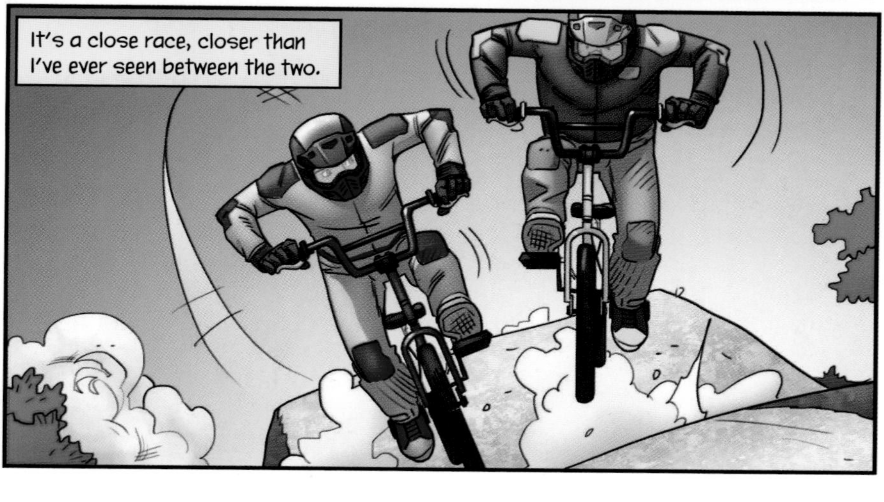
It's a close race, closer than I've ever seen between the two.

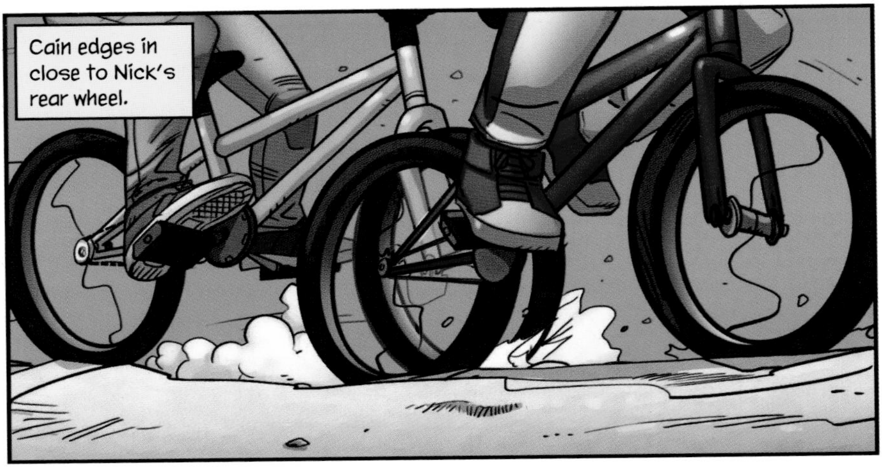
Cain edges in close to Nick's rear wheel.

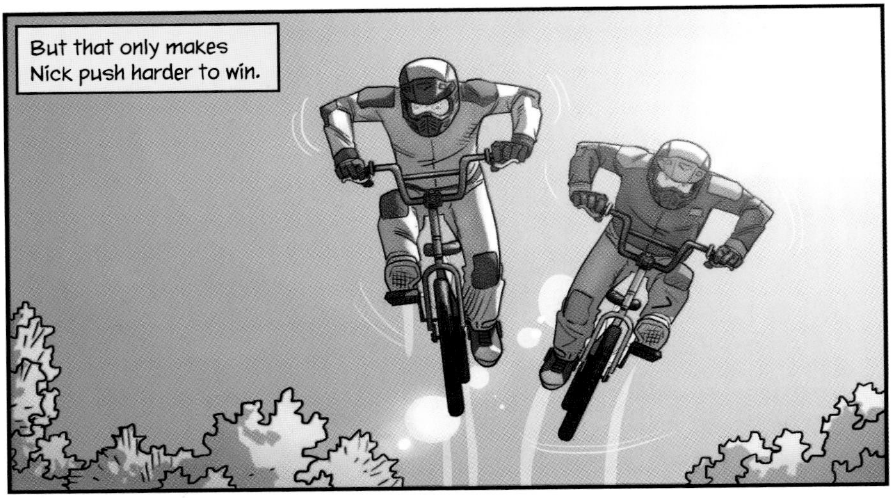
But that only makes Nick push harder to win.

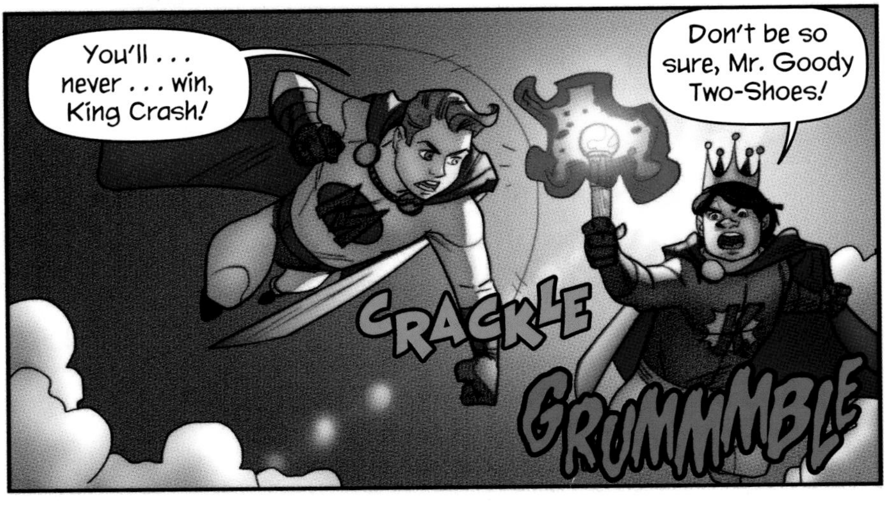
You'll . . . never . . . win, King Crash!
Don't be so sure, Mr. Goody Two-Shoes!
CRACKLE
GRUMMMBLE

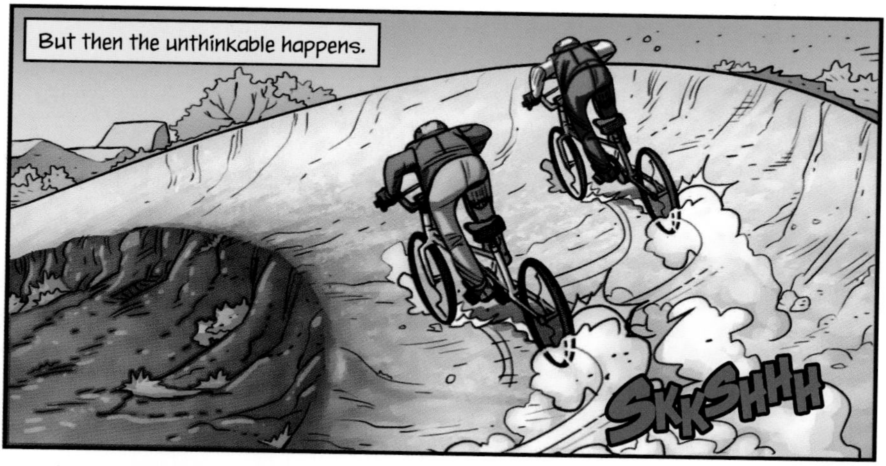
But then the unthinkable happens.
SKKSHHH

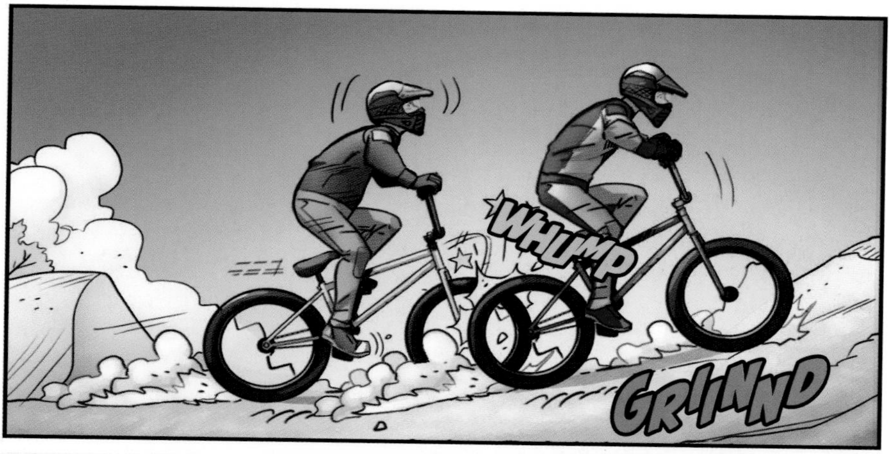
WHUMP
GRIINND

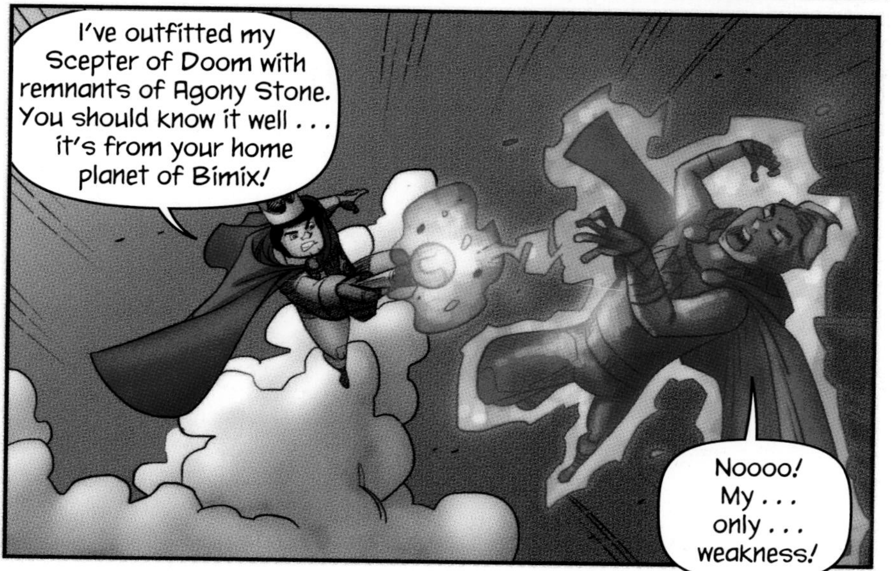
I've outfitted my Scepter of Doom with remnants of Agony Stone. You should know it well . . . it's from your home planet of Bimix!
Noooo! My . . . only . . . weakness!

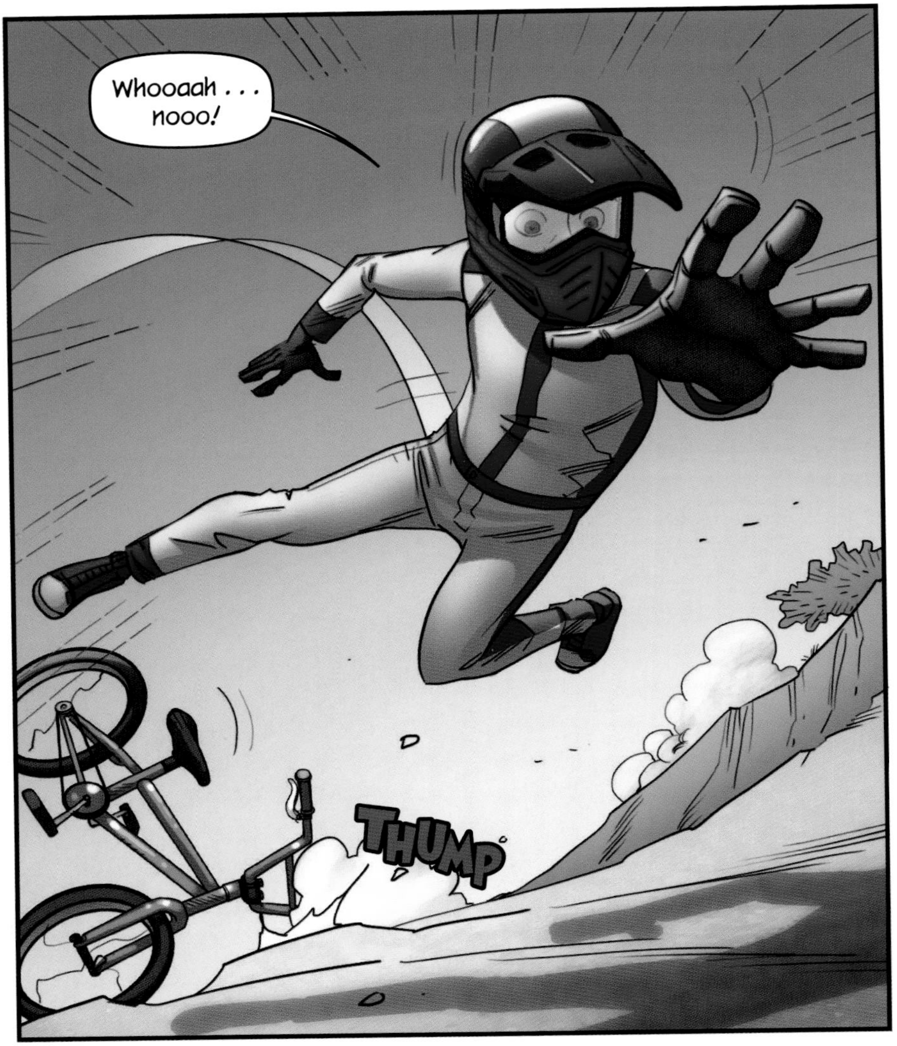
Whooaah . . .
nooo!
THUMP

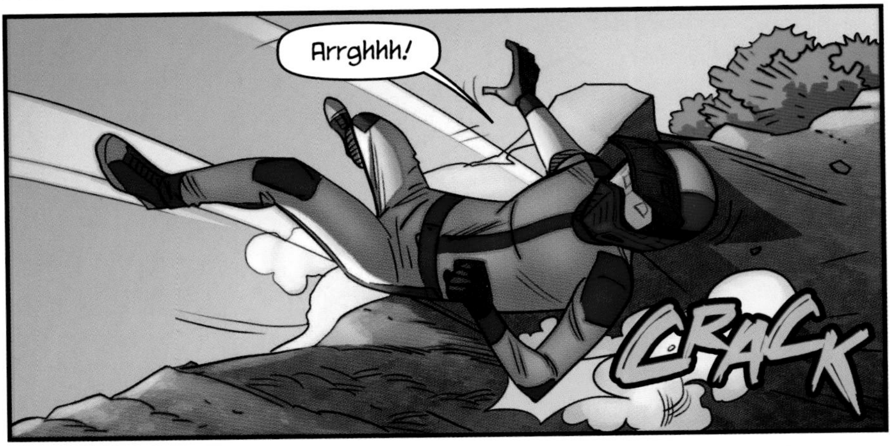
Arrghhh!
CRACK

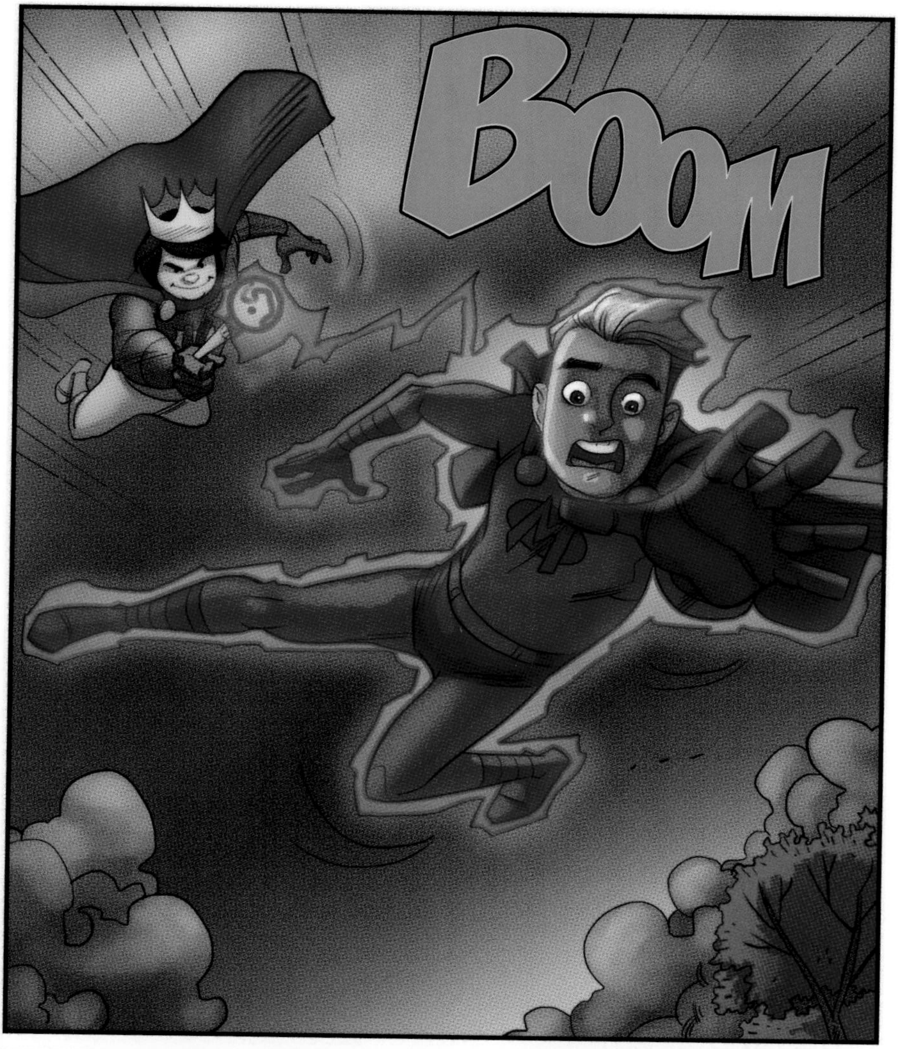
BOOM

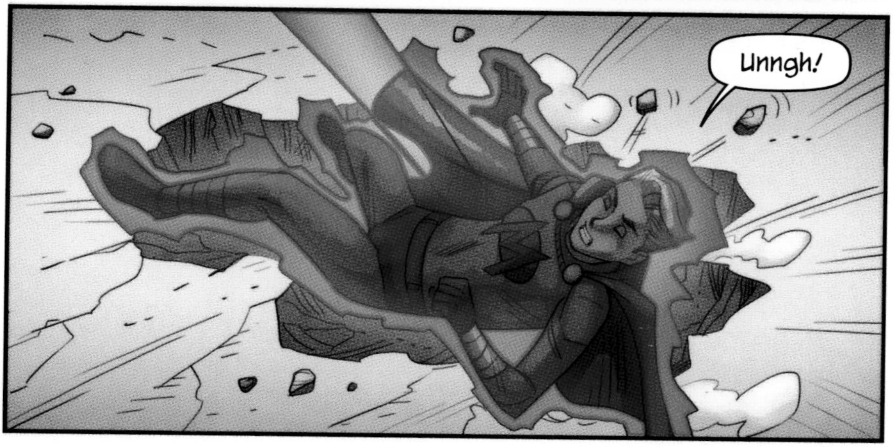
Unngh!

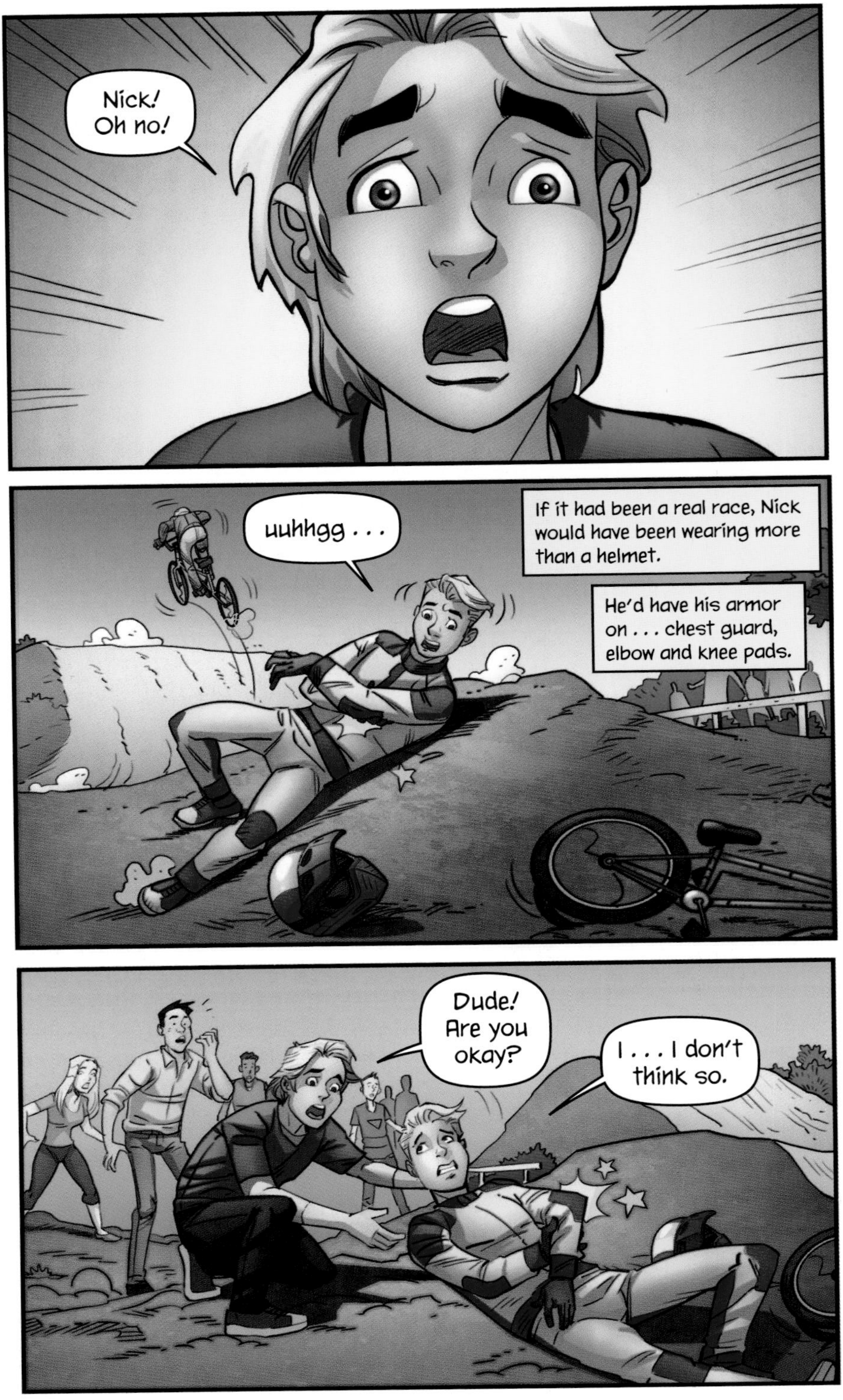
Nick! Oh no!
uuhhgg . . .
If it had been a real race, Nick would have been wearing more than a helmet.
He'd have his armor on . . . chest guard, elbow and knee pads.
Dude! Are you okay?
I . . . I don't think so.

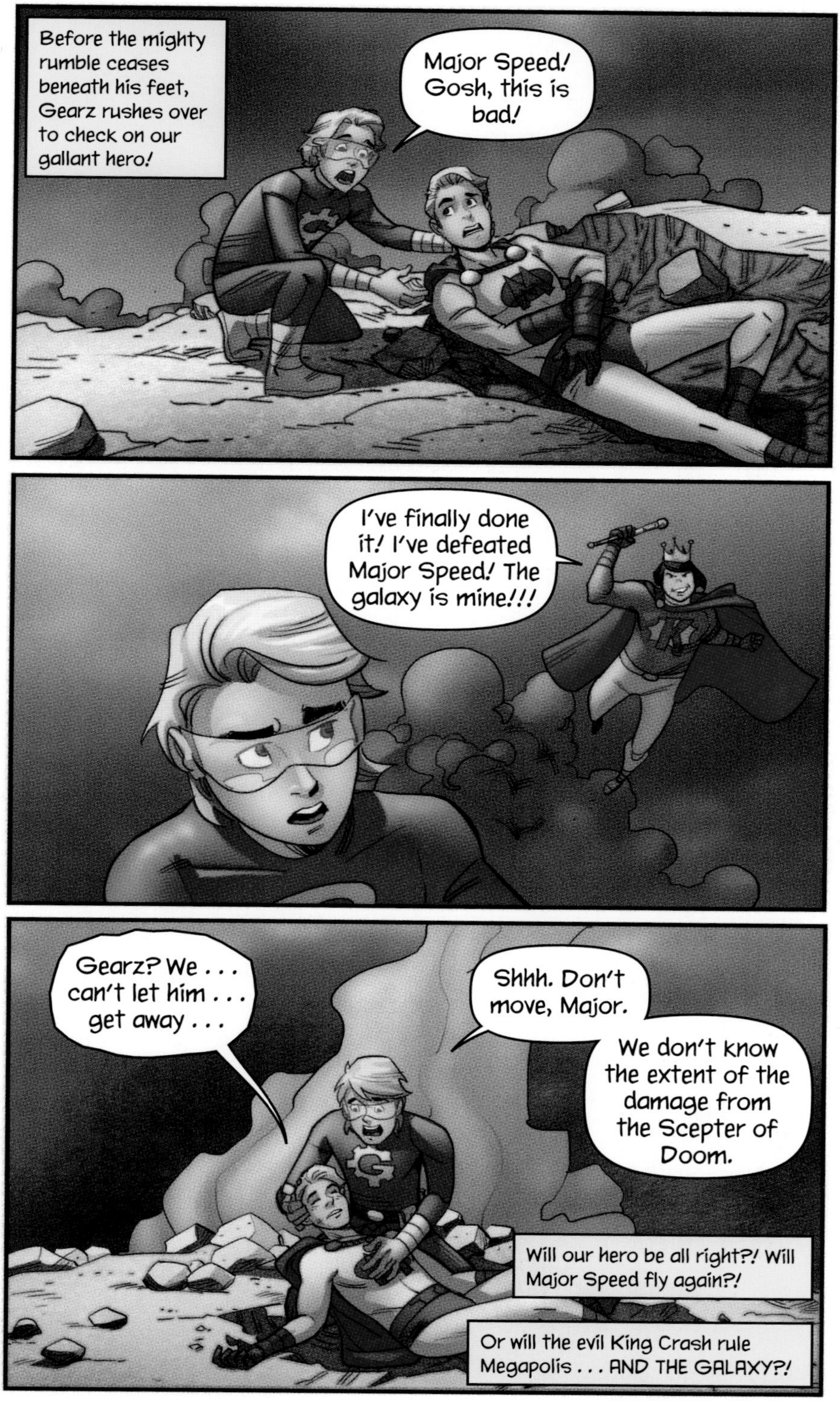
Before the mighty rumble ceases beneath his feet, Gearz rushes over to check on our gallant hero!
Major Speed! Gosh, this is bad!
I've finally done it! I've defeated Major Speed! The galaxy is mine!!!
Gearz? We . . . can't let him . . . get away . . .
Shhh. Don't move, Major.
We don't know the extent of the damage from the Scepter of Doom.
Will our hero be all right?! Will Major Speed fly again?!
Or will the evil King Crash rule Megapolis . . . AND THE GALAXY?!

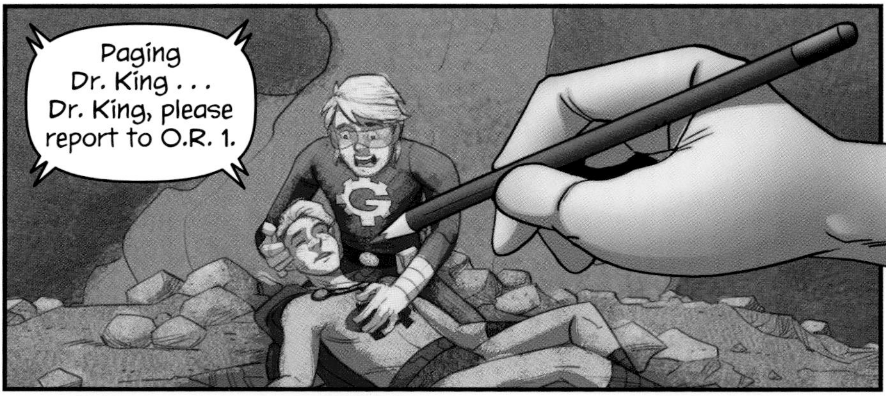
Paging Dr. King . . . Dr. King, please report to O.R. 1.

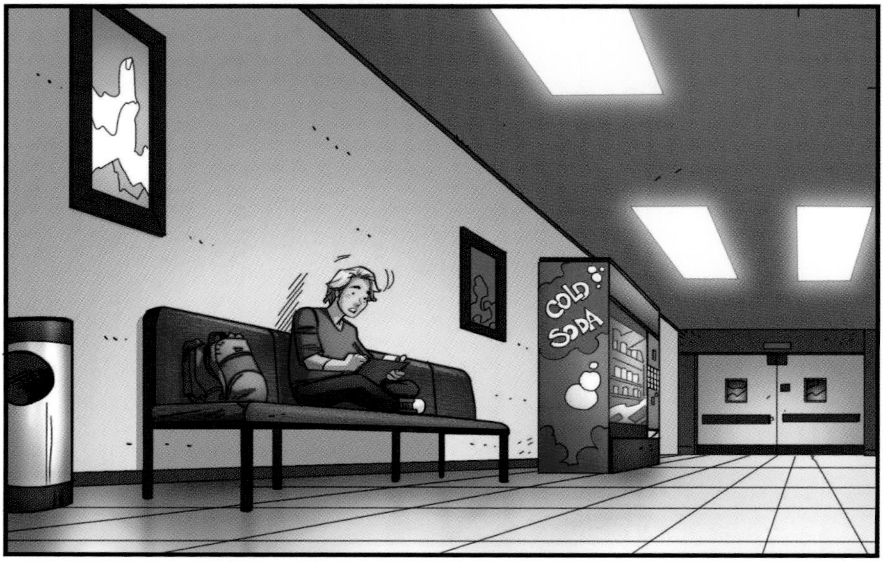
COLD SODA

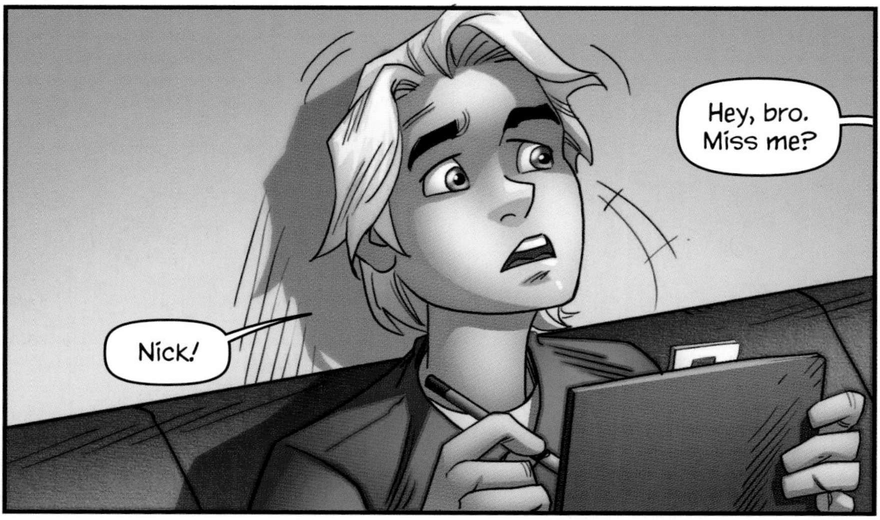
Hey, bro. Miss me?
Nick!

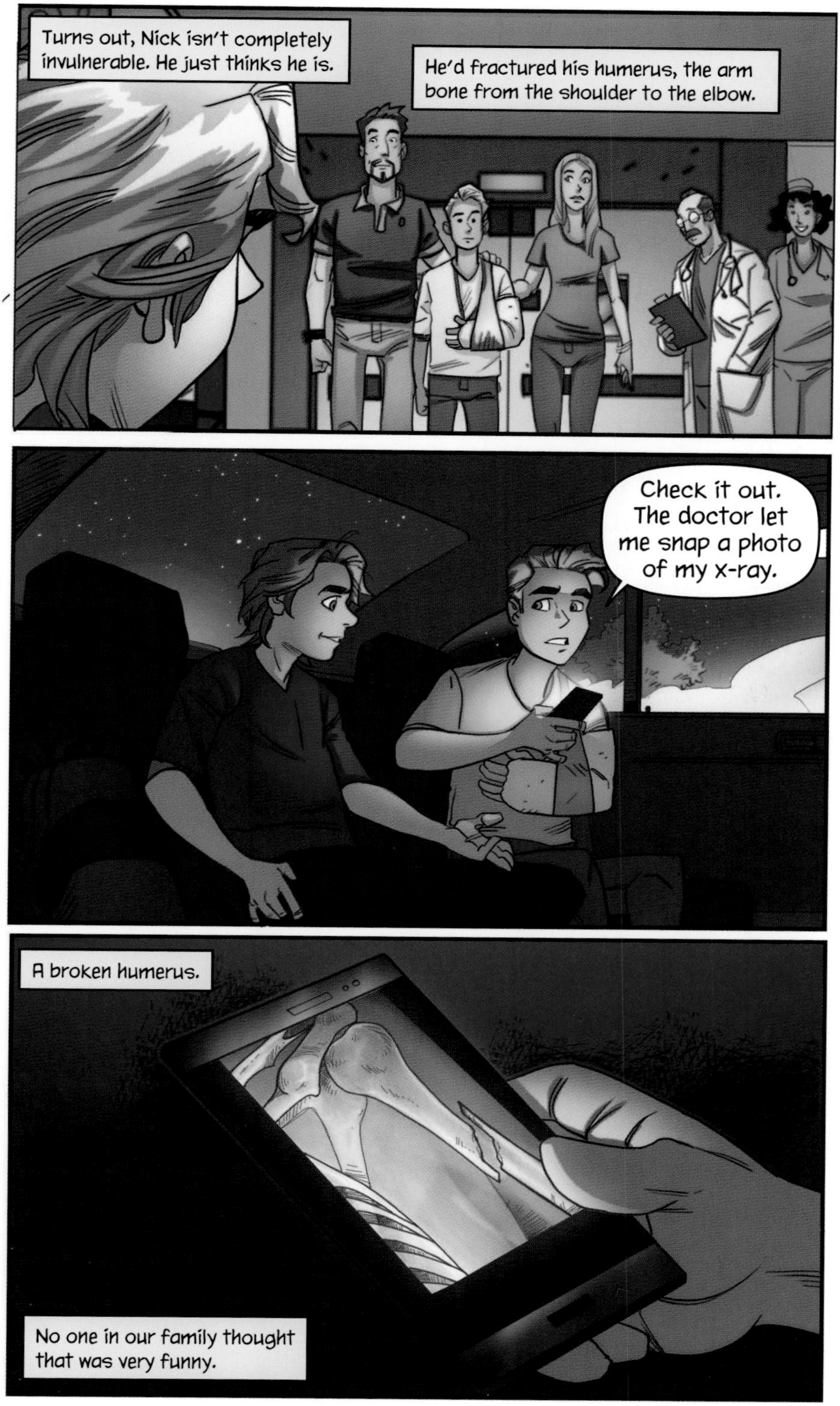
Turns out, Nick isn't completely invulnerable. He just thinks he is.
He'd fractured his humerus, the arm bone from the shoulder to the elbow.
Check it out. The doctor let me snap a photo of my x-ray.
A broken humerus.
No one in our family thought that was very funny.

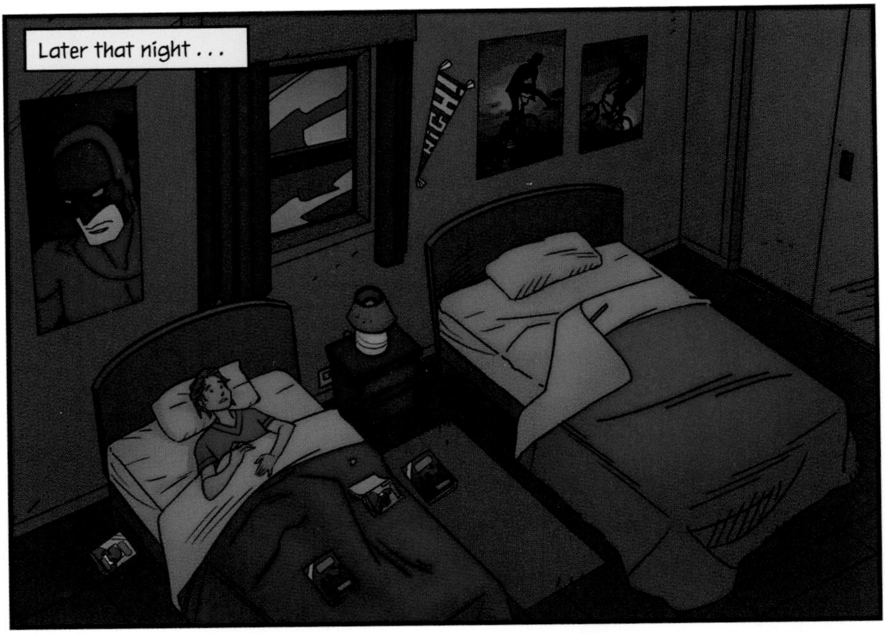
Later that night . . .
HIGH!

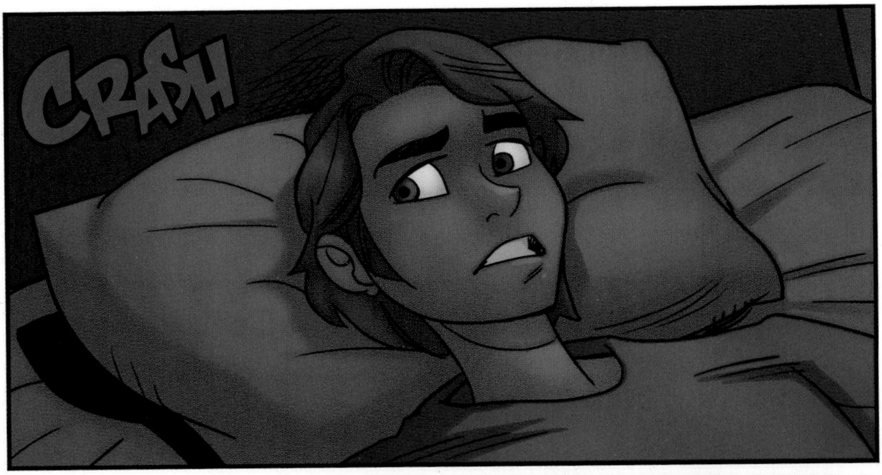
CRASH

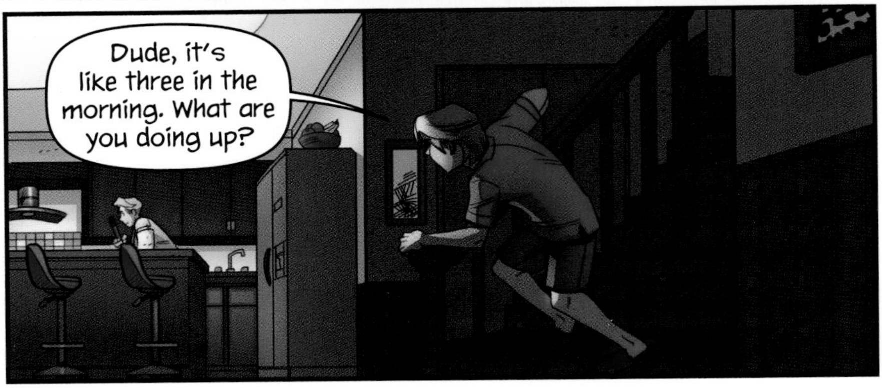
Dude, it's like three in the morning. What are you doing up?

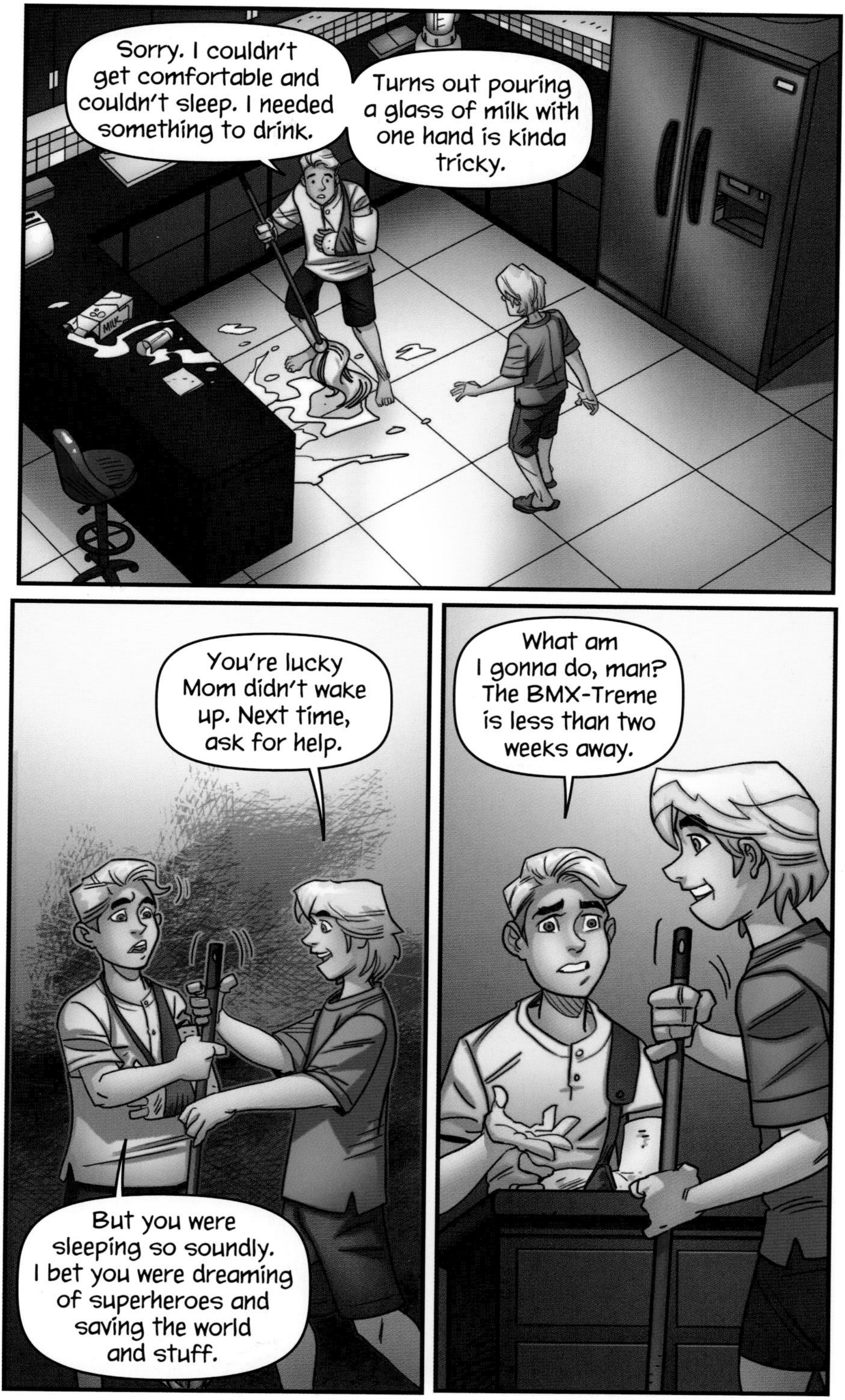
Sorry. I couldn't get comfortable and couldn't sleep. I needed something to drink.
Turns out pouring a glass of milk with one hand is kinda tricky.
MILK
You're lucky Mom didn't wake up. Next time, ask for help.
But you were sleeping so soundly. I bet you were dreaming of superheroes and saving the world and stuff.
What am I gonna do, man? The BMX-Treme is less than two weeks away.

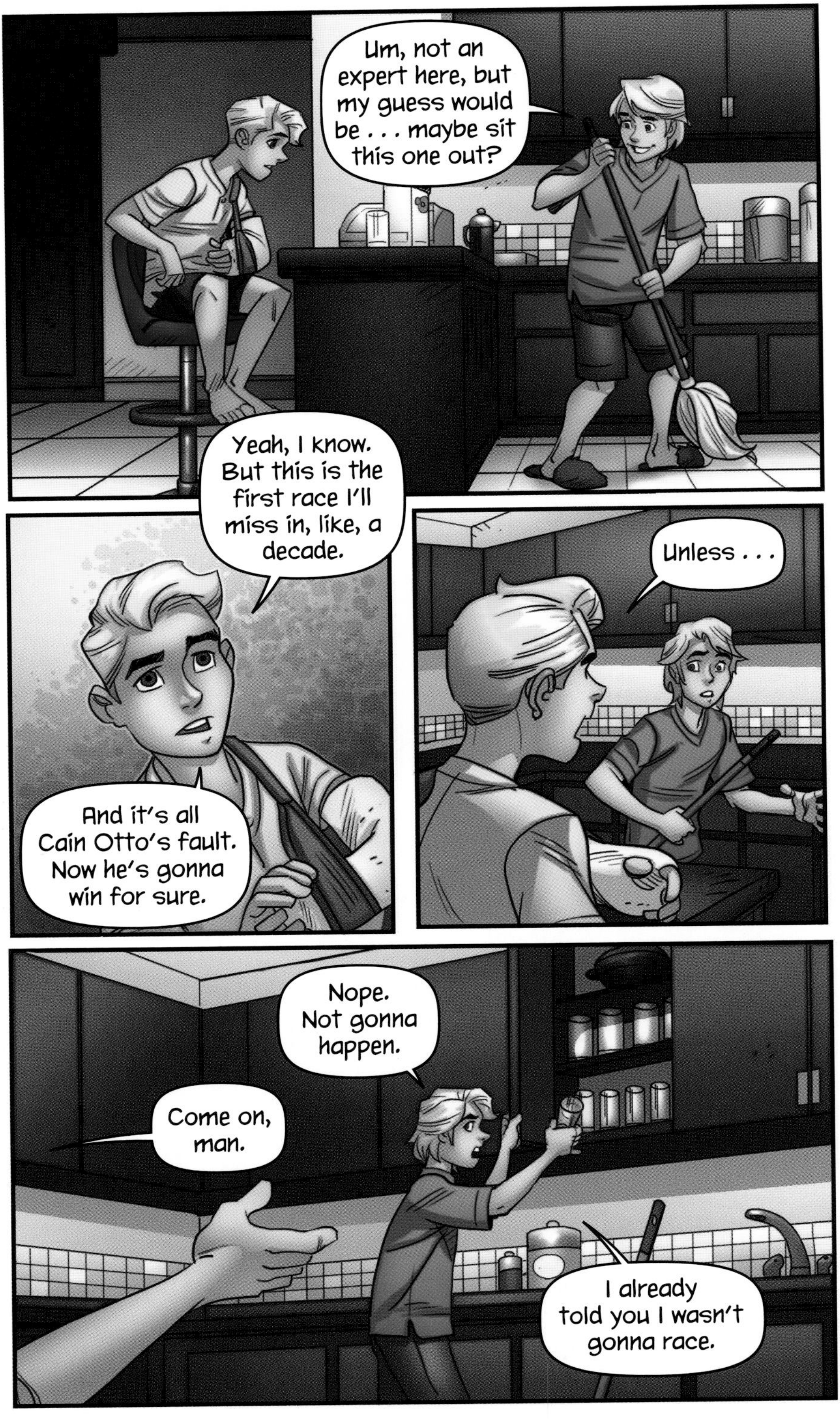
Um, not an expert here, but my guess would be . . . maybe sit this one out?
Yeah, I know. But this is the first race I'll miss in, like, a decade.
And it's all Cain Otto's fault. Now he's gonna win for sure.
Unless . . .
Nope. Not gonna happen.
Come on, man.
I already told you I wasn't gonna race.

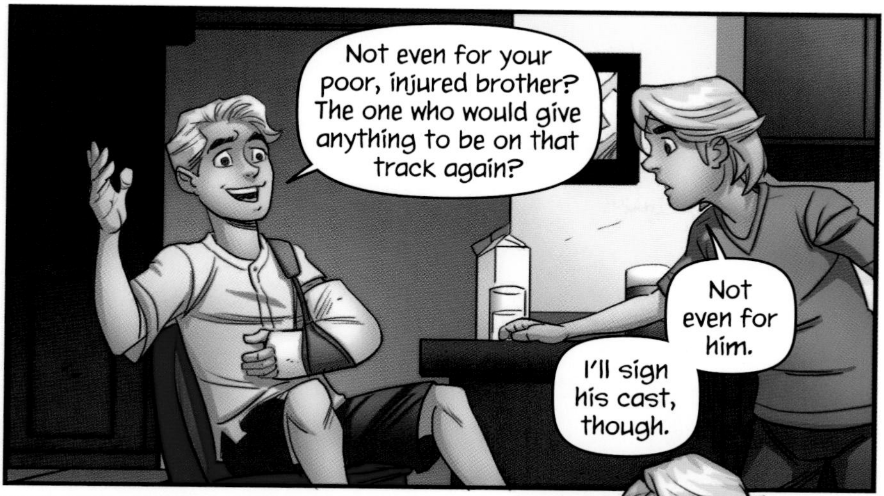
Not even for your poor, injured brother? The one who would give anything to be on that track again?
Not even for him.
I'll sign his cast, though.

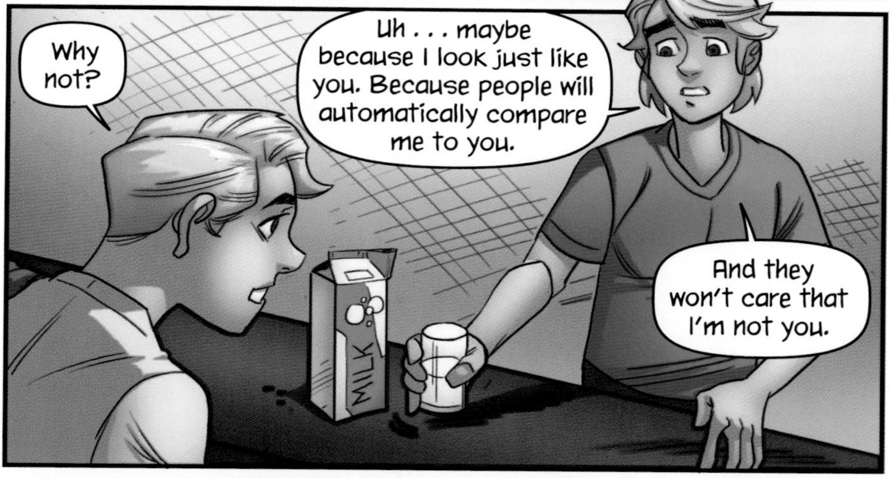
Why not?
Uh . . . maybe because I look just like you. Because people will automatically compare me to you.
And they won't care that I'm not you.
MILK

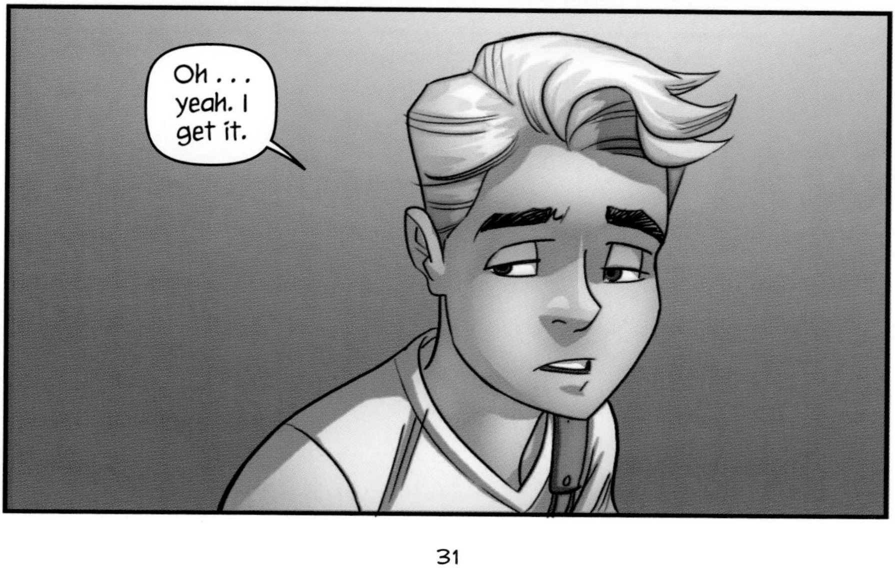
Oh . . . yeah. I get it.

Meanwhile, back at Major Speed HQ . . .

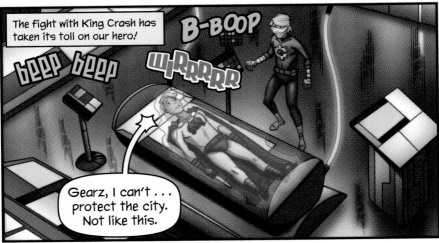

The fight with King Crash has taken its toll on our hero!

B-BOOP

beep beep

WiRRRRR

Gearz, I can't . . . protect the city. Not like this.

The good citizens of Megapolis . . . now look to you, Gearz.

Whoa, really?

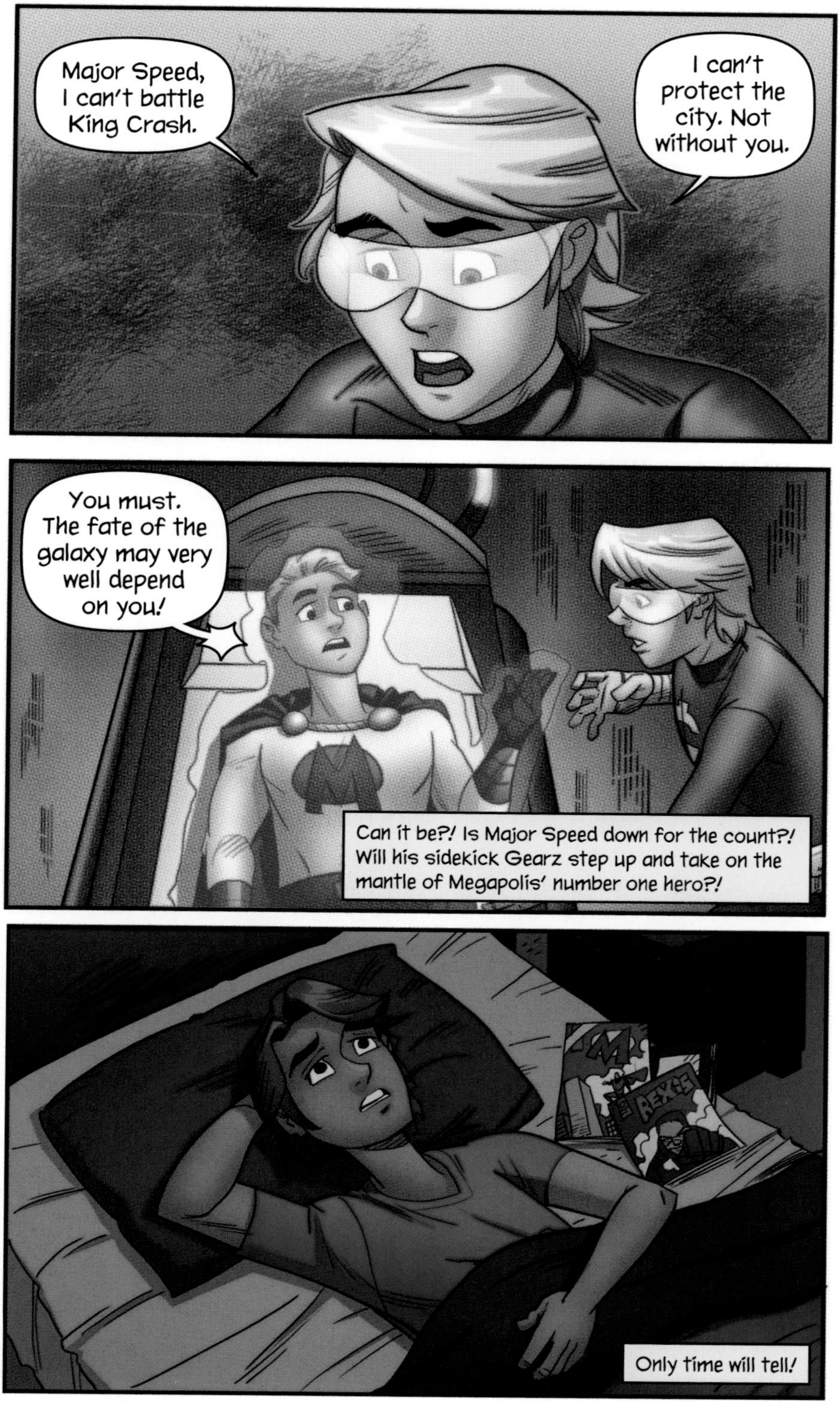
Major Speed, I can't battle King Crash.
I can't protect the city. Not without you.
You must. The fate of the galaxy may very well depend on you!
Can it be?! Is Major Speed down for the count?! Will his sidekick Gearz step up and take on the mantle of Megapolis' number one hero?!
Only time will tell!

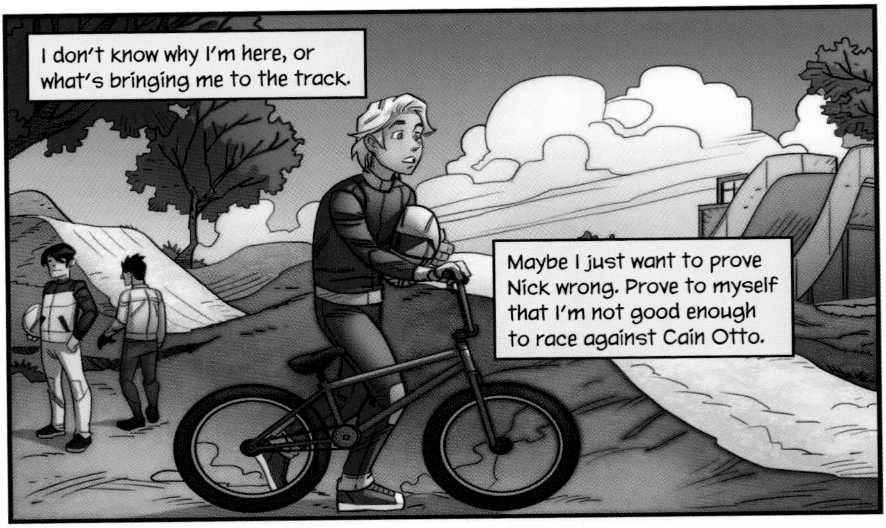
I don't know why I'm here, or what's bringing me to the track.
Maybe I just want to prove Nick wrong. Prove to myself that I'm not good enough to race against Cain Otto.

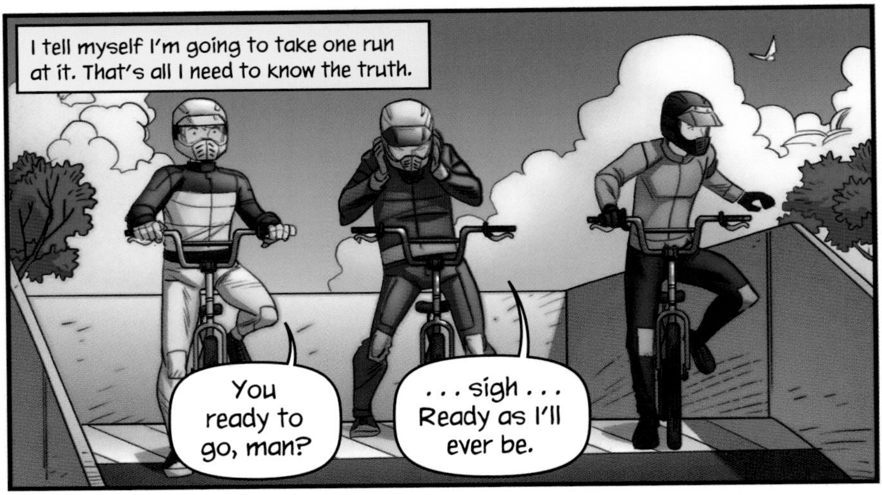
I tell myself I'm going to take one run at it. That's all I need to know the truth.
You ready to go, man?
. . . sigh . . . Ready as I'll ever be.

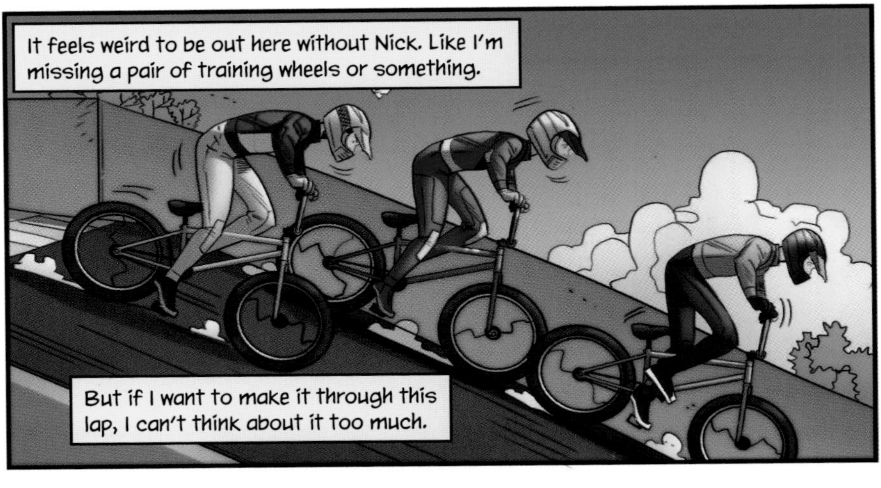
It feels weird to be out here without Nick. Like I'm missing a pair of training wheels or something.
But if I want to make it through this lap, I can't think about it too much.

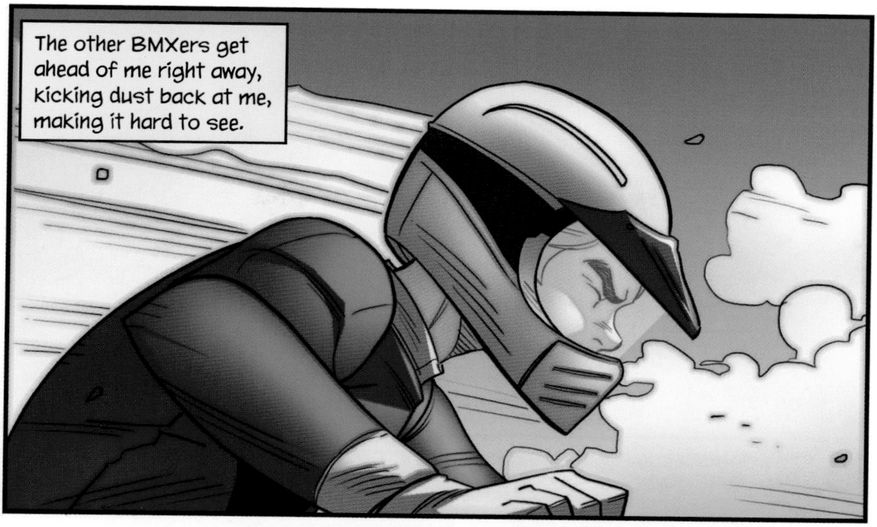
The other BMXers get ahead of me right away, kicking dust back at me, making it hard to see.

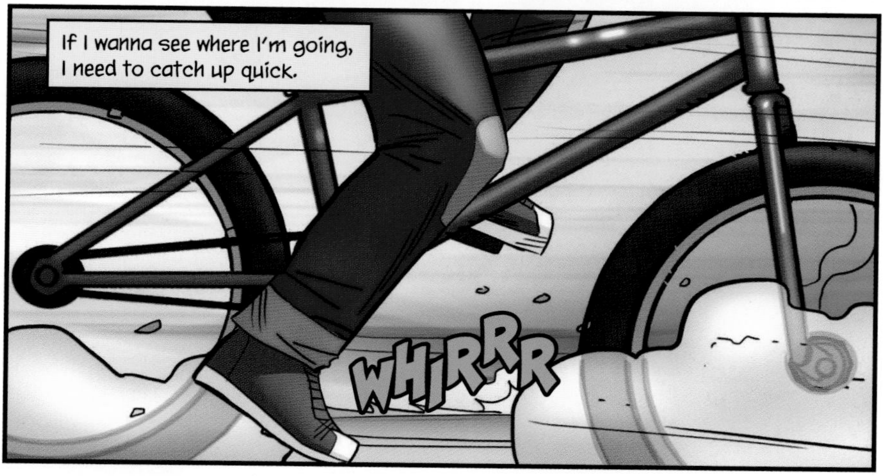
If I wanna see where I'm going, I need to catch up quick.
WHIRRR

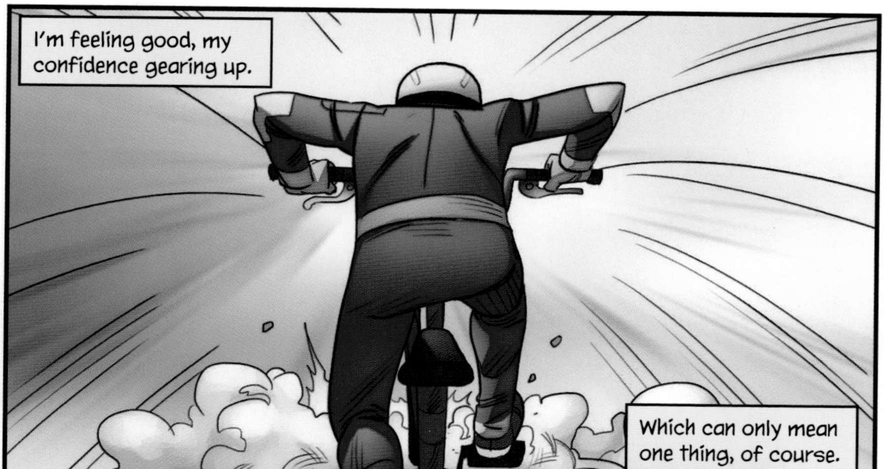
I'm feeling good, my confidence gearing up.
Which can only mean one thing, of course.

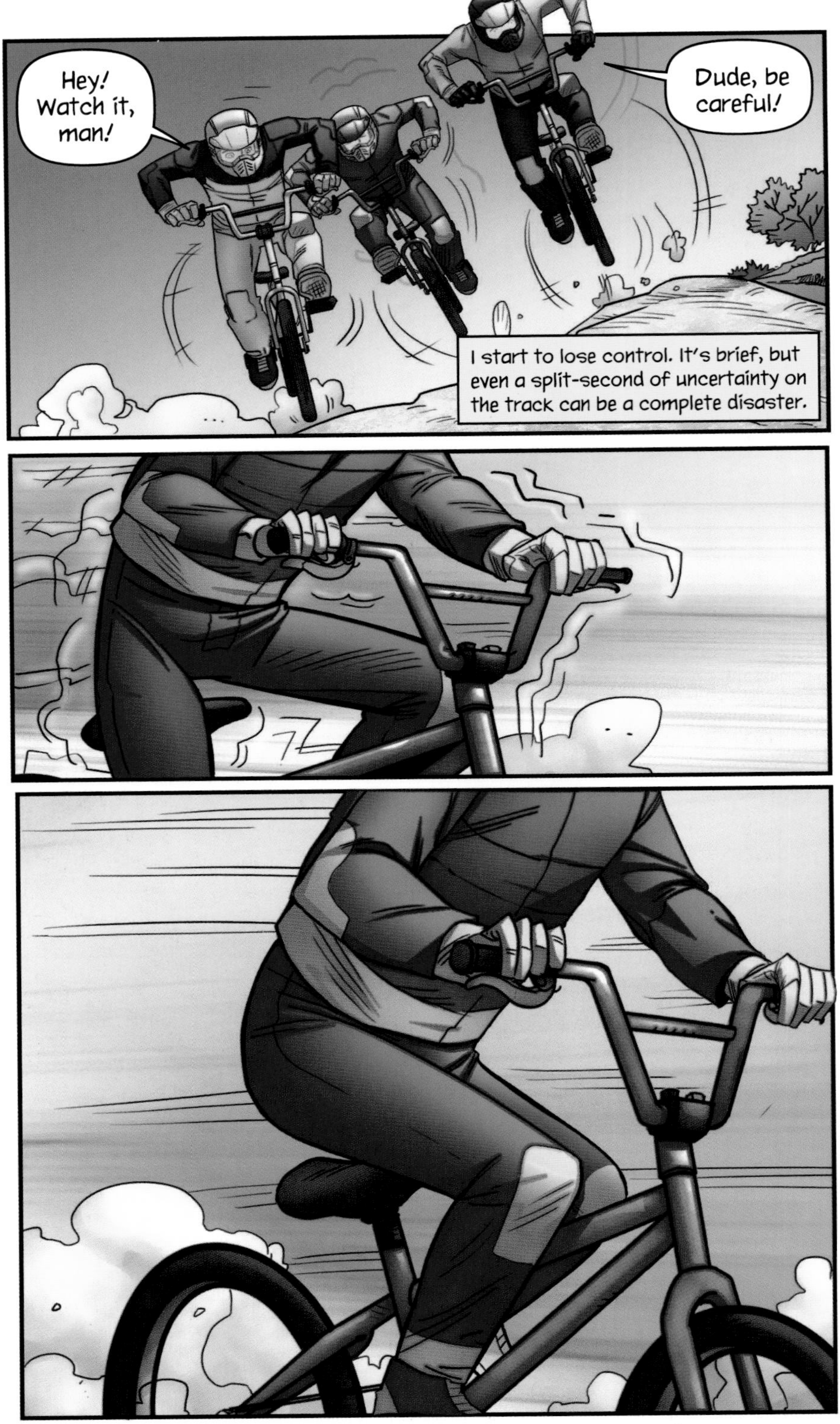
Hey! Watch it, man!
Dude, be careful!
I start to lose control. It's brief, but even a split-second of uncertainty on the track can be a complete disaster.

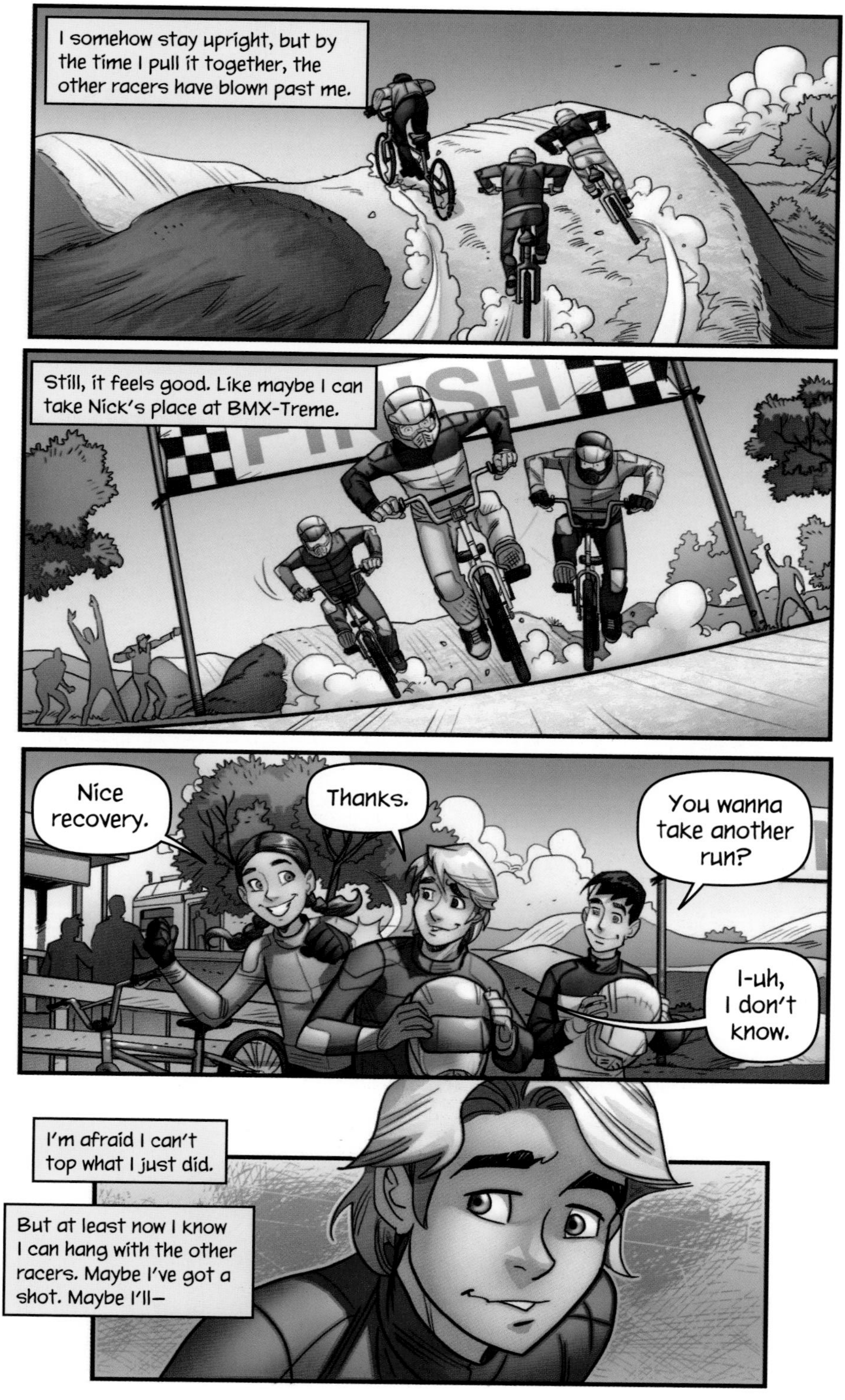
I somehow stay upright, but by the time I pull it together, the other racers have blown past me.
FINISH
Still, it feels good. Like maybe I can take Nick's place at BMX-Treme.
Nice recovery.
Thanks.
You wanna take another run?
I-uh, I don't know.
I'm afraid I can't top what I just did.
But at least now I know I can hang with the other racers. Maybe I've got a shot. Maybe I'll—

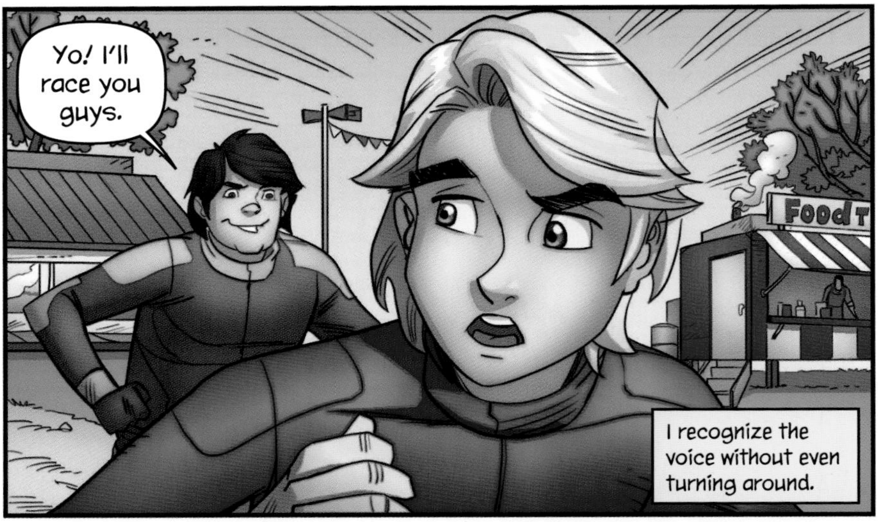
Yo! I'll race you guys.
I recognize the voice without even turning around.
Food

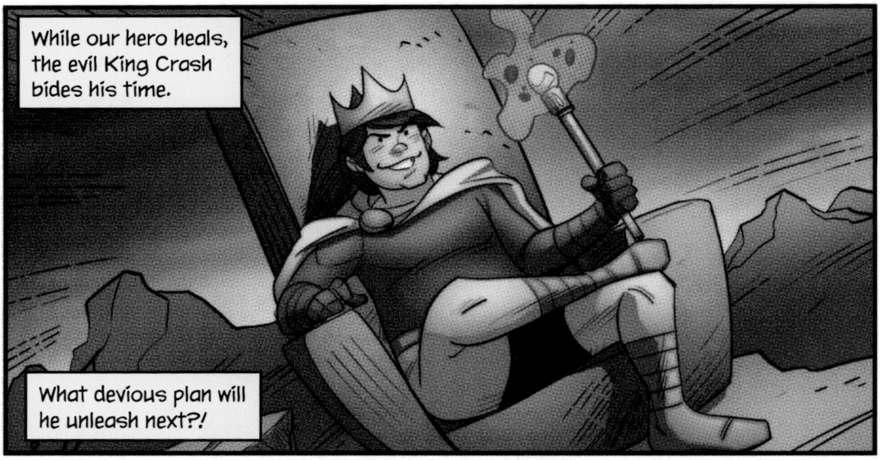
While our hero heals, the evil King Crash bides his time.
What devious plan will he unleash next?!

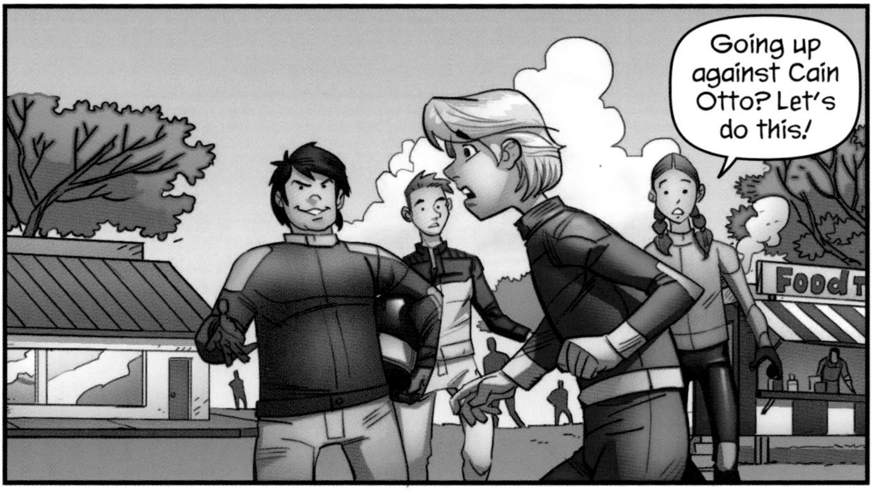
Going up against Cain Otto? Let's do this!
Food

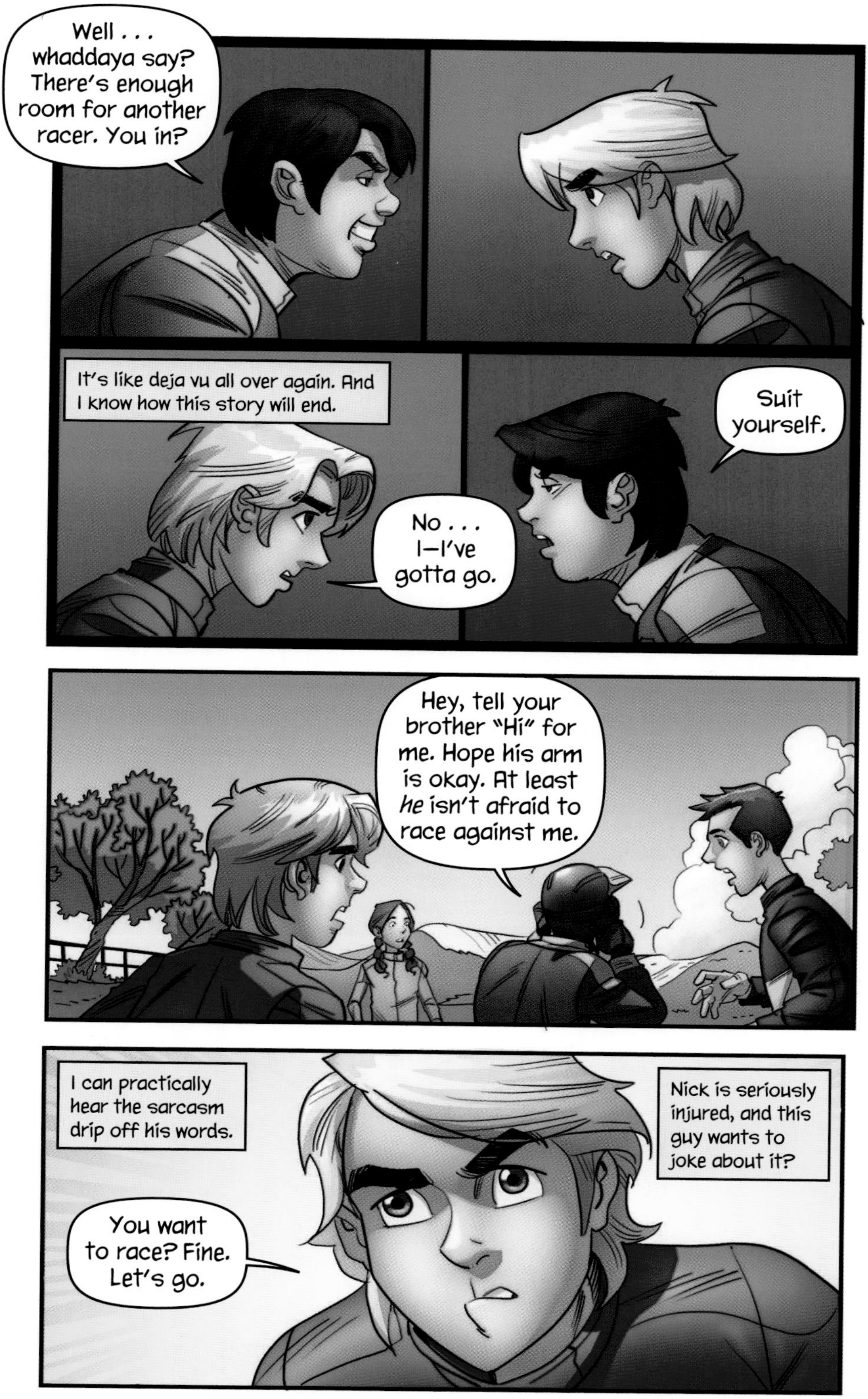
Well . . . whaddaya say? There's enough room for another racer. You in?
It's like deja vu all over again. And I know how this story will end.
No . . . I—I've gotta go.
Suit yourself.
Hey, tell your brother "Hi" for me. Hope his arm is okay. At least *he* isn't afraid to race against me.
I can practically hear the sarcasm drip off his words.
Nick is seriously injured, and this guy wants to joke about it?
You want to race? Fine. Let's go.

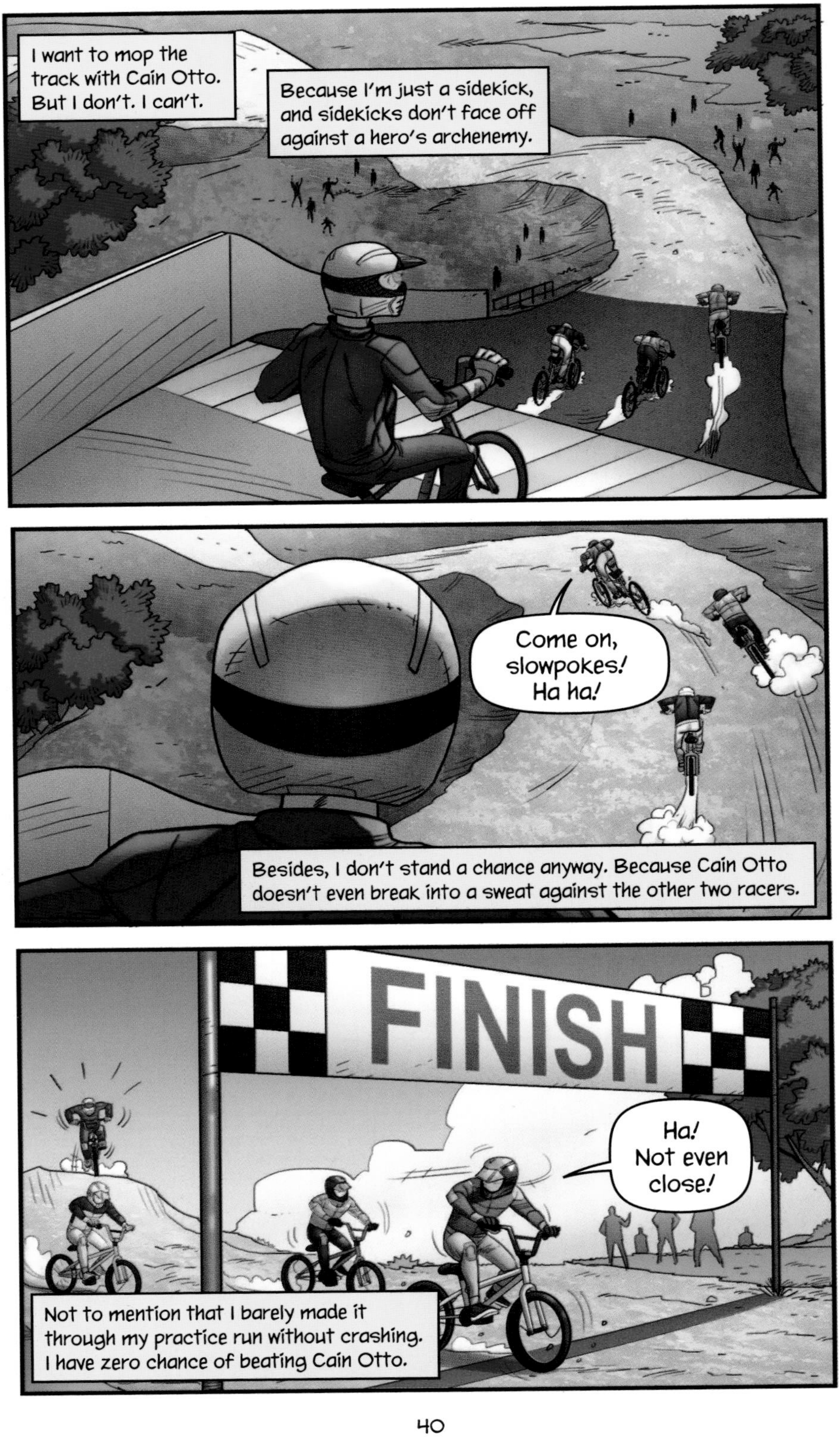
I want to mop the track with Cain Otto. But I don't. I can't.
Because I'm just a sidekick, and sidekicks don't face off against a hero's archenemy.
Come on, slowpokes! Ha ha!
Besides, I don't stand a chance anyway. Because Cain Otto doesn't even break into a sweat against the other two racers.
FINISH
Ha! Not even close!
Not to mention that I barely made it through my practice run without crashing. I have zero chance of beating Cain Otto.

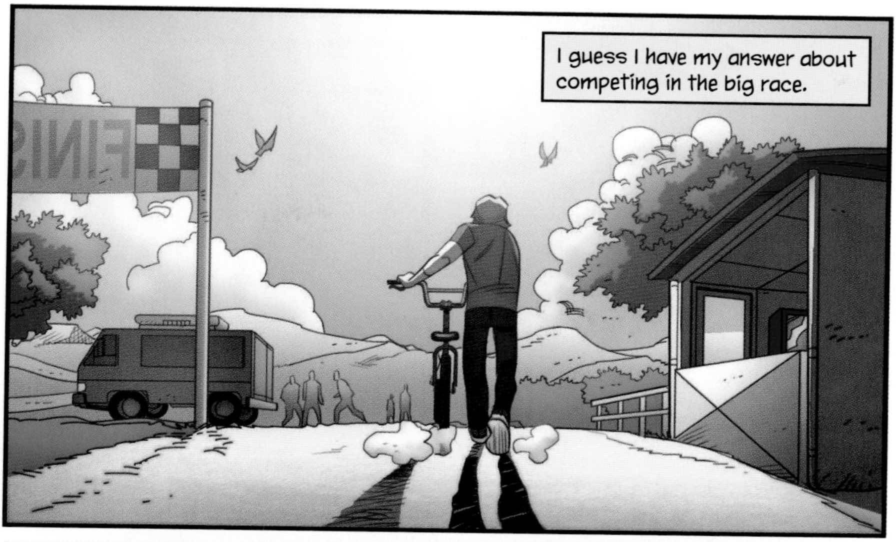
I guess I have my answer about competing in the big race.

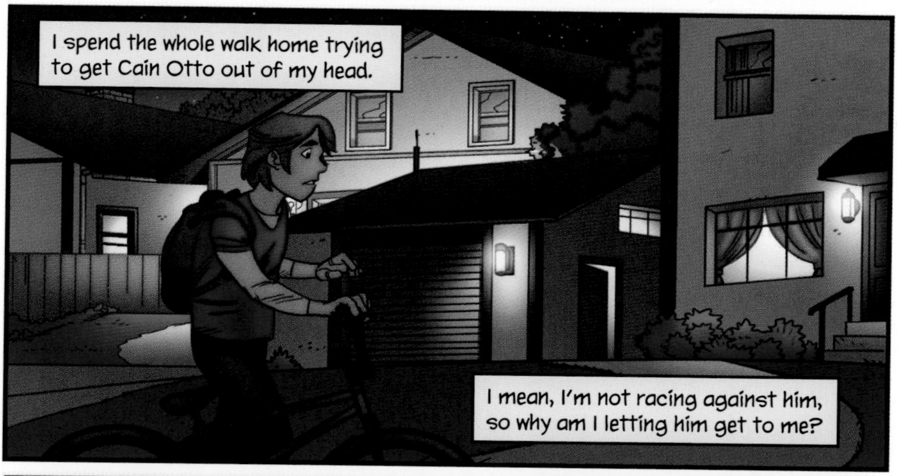
I spend the whole walk home trying to get Cain Otto out of my head.
I mean, I'm not racing against him, so why am I letting him get to me?

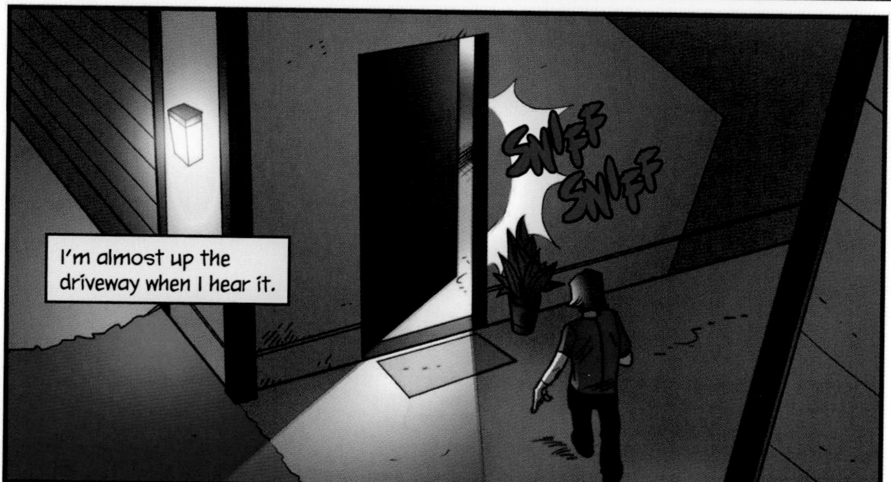
SNIFF
SNIFF
I'm almost up the driveway when I hear it.

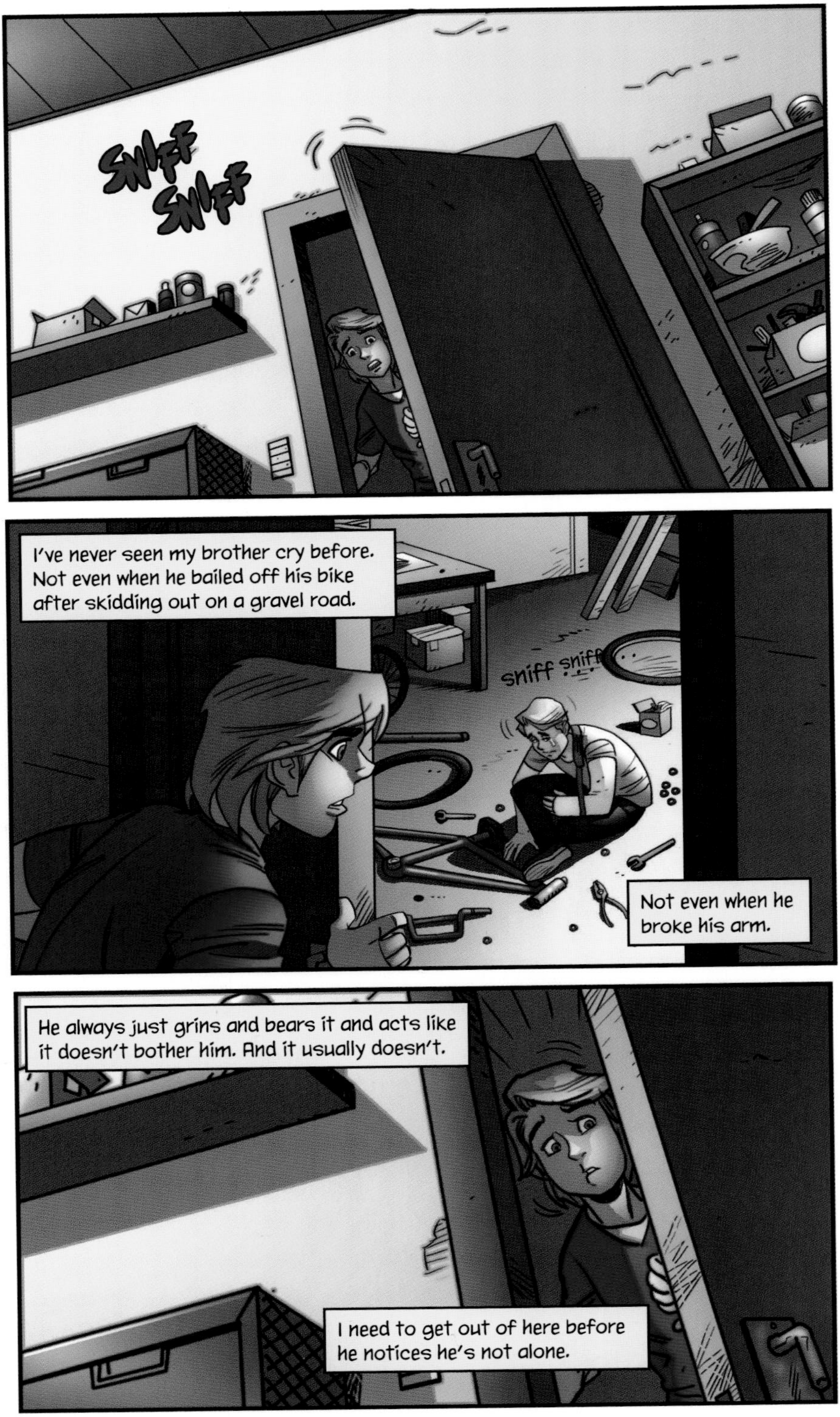
SNIFF
SNIFF
I've never seen my brother cry before. Not even when he bailed off his bike after skidding out on a gravel road.
sniff sniff
Not even when he broke his arm.
He always just grins and bears it and acts like it doesn't bother him. And it usually doesn't.
I need to get out of here before he notices he's not alone.

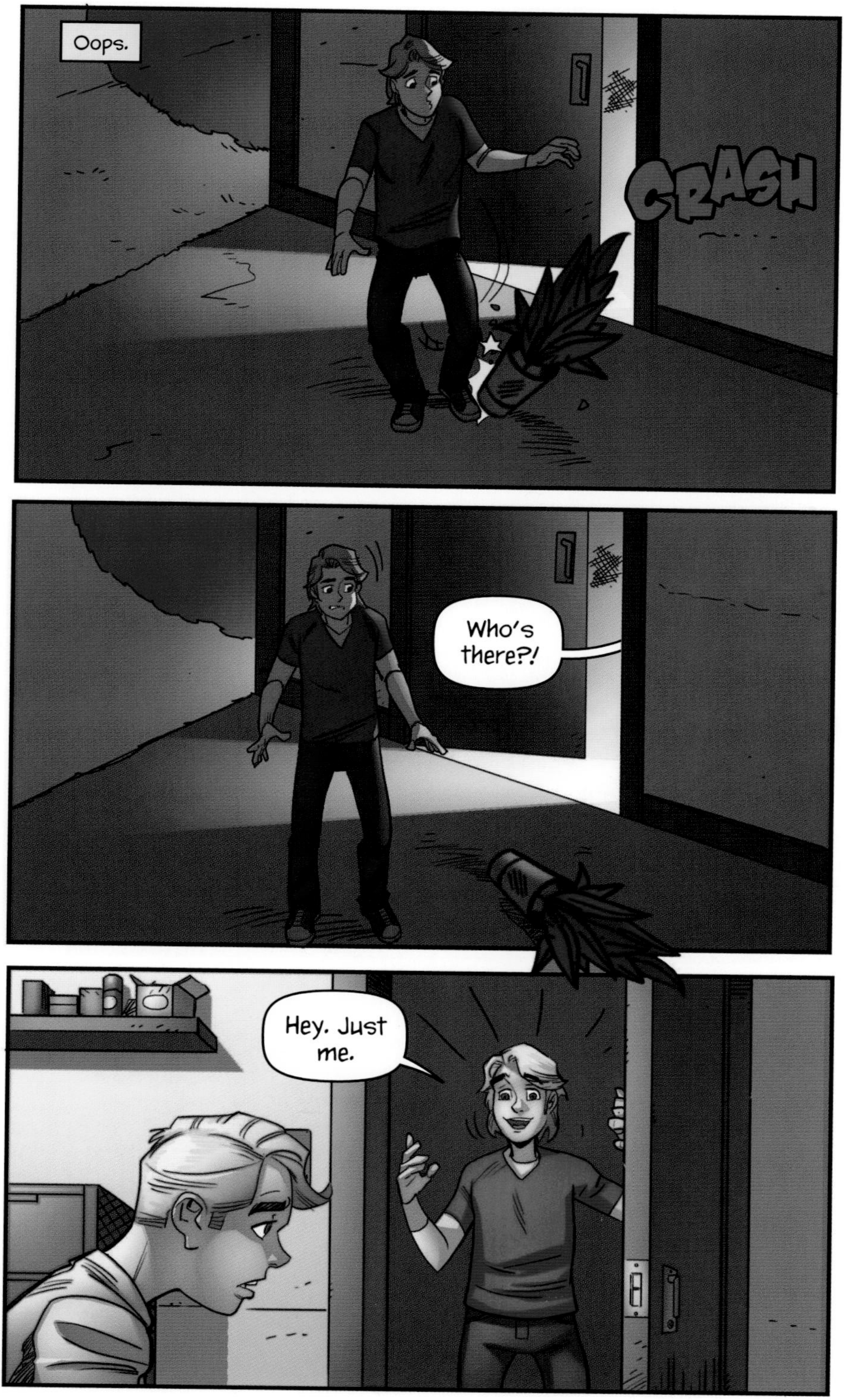
Oops.
CRASH
Who's there?!
Hey. Just me.

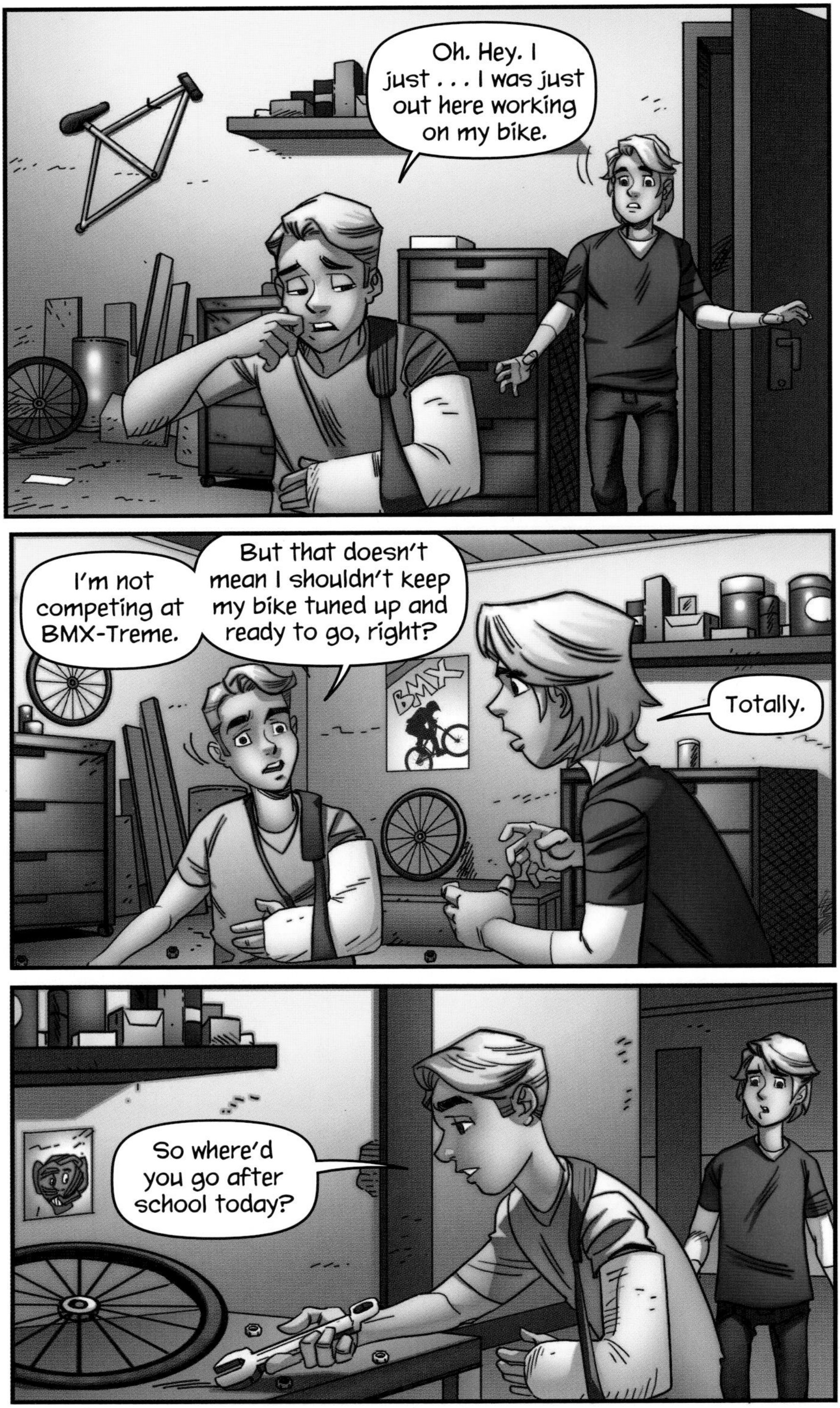
Oh. Hey. I just . . . I was just out here working on my bike.
I'm not competing at BMX-Treme.
But that doesn't mean I shouldn't keep my bike tuned up and ready to go, right?
BMX
Totally.
So where'd you go after school today?

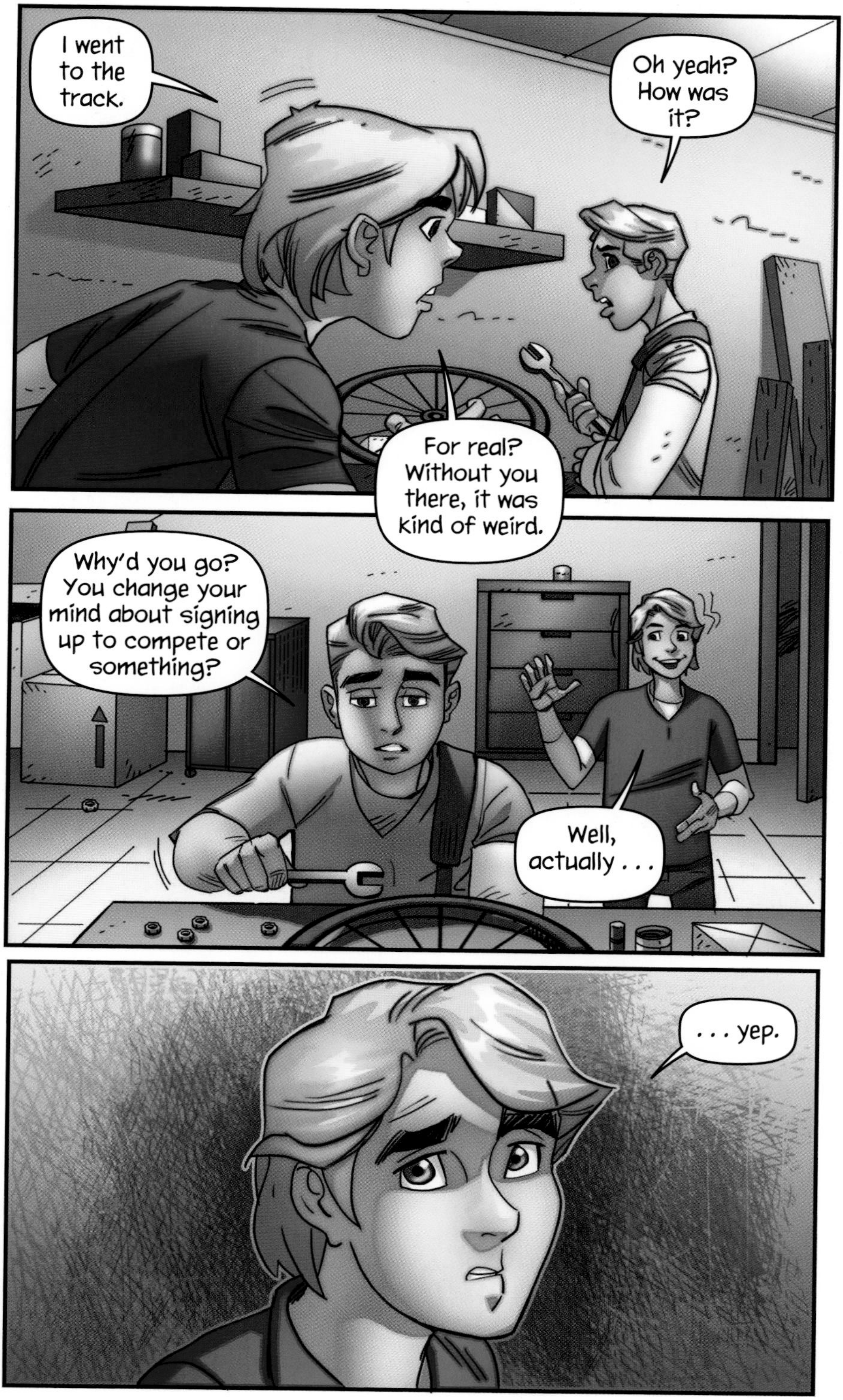
I went to the track.
Oh yeah? How was it?
For real? Without you there, it was kind of weird.
Why'd you go? You change your mind about signing up to compete or something?
Well, actually . . .
. . . yep.

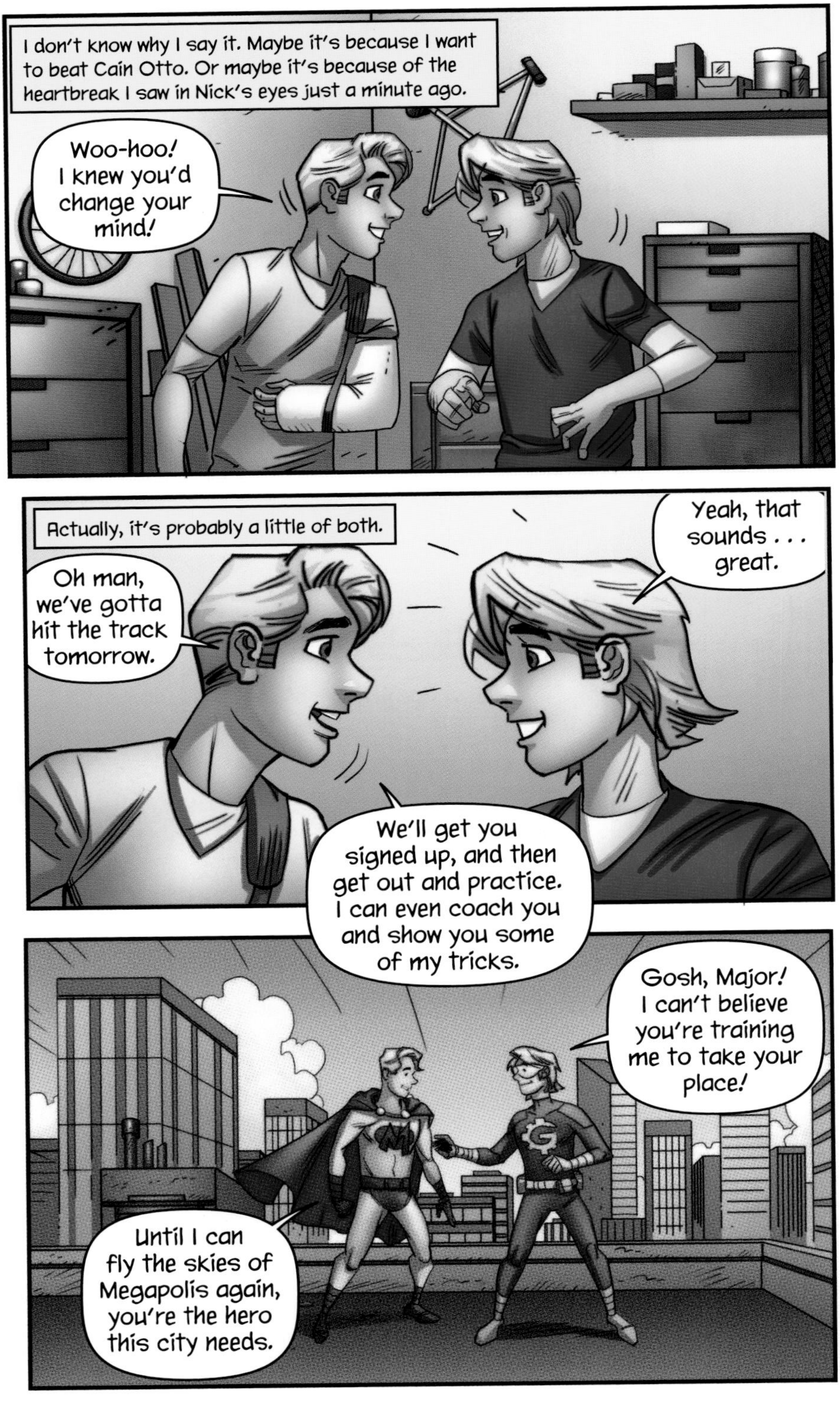
I don't know why I say it. Maybe it's because I want to beat Cain Otto. Or maybe it's because of the heartbreak I saw in Nick's eyes just a minute ago.
Woo-hoo! I knew you'd change your mind!
Actually, it's probably a little of both.
Oh man, we've gotta hit the track tomorrow.
Yeah, that sounds . . . great.
We'll get you signed up, and then get out and practice. I can even coach you and show you some of my tricks.
Gosh, Major! I can't believe you're training me to take your place!
Until I can fly the skies of Megapolis again, you're the hero this city needs.

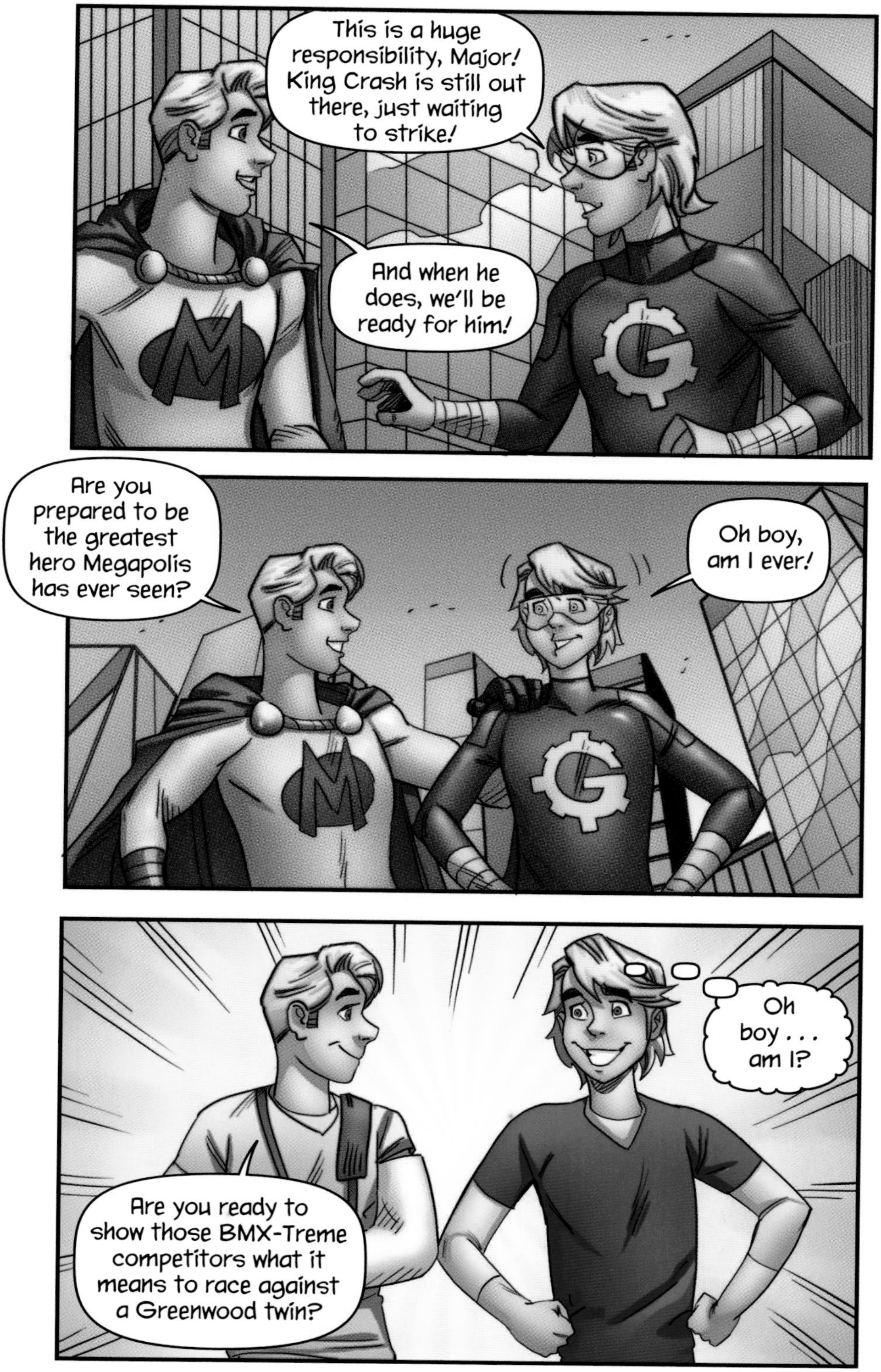
This is a huge responsibility, Major! King Crash is still out there, just waiting to strike!
And when he does, we'll be ready for him!
Are you prepared to be the greatest hero Megapolis has ever seen?
Oh boy, am I ever!
Oh boy . . . am I?
Are you ready to show those BMX-Treme competitors what it means to race against a Greenwood twin?

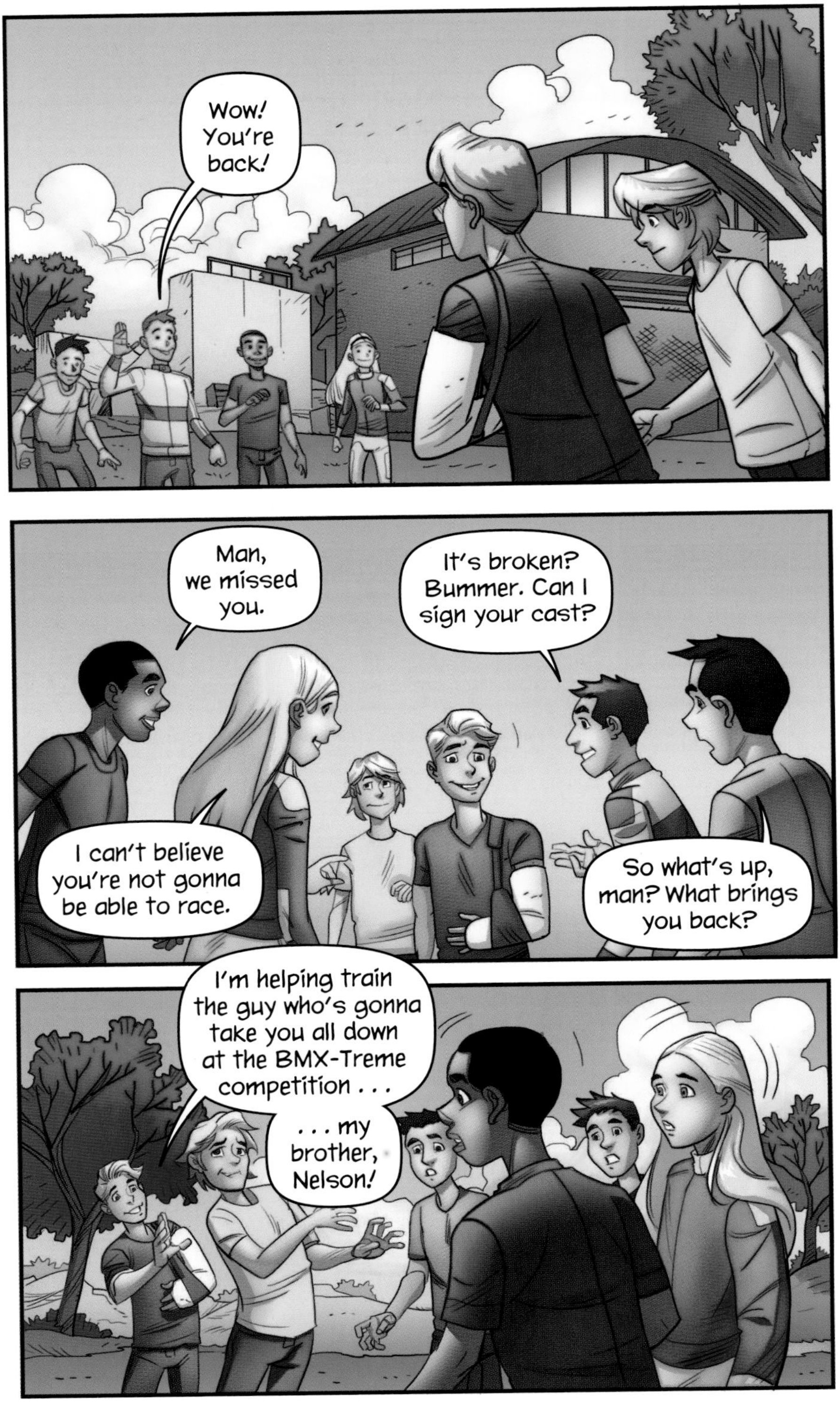
Wow! You're back!
Man, we missed you.
It's broken? Bummer. Can I sign your cast?
I can't believe you're not gonna be able to race.
So what's up, man? What brings you back?
I'm helping train the guy who's gonna take you all down at the BMX-Treme competition . . .
. . . my brother, Nelson!

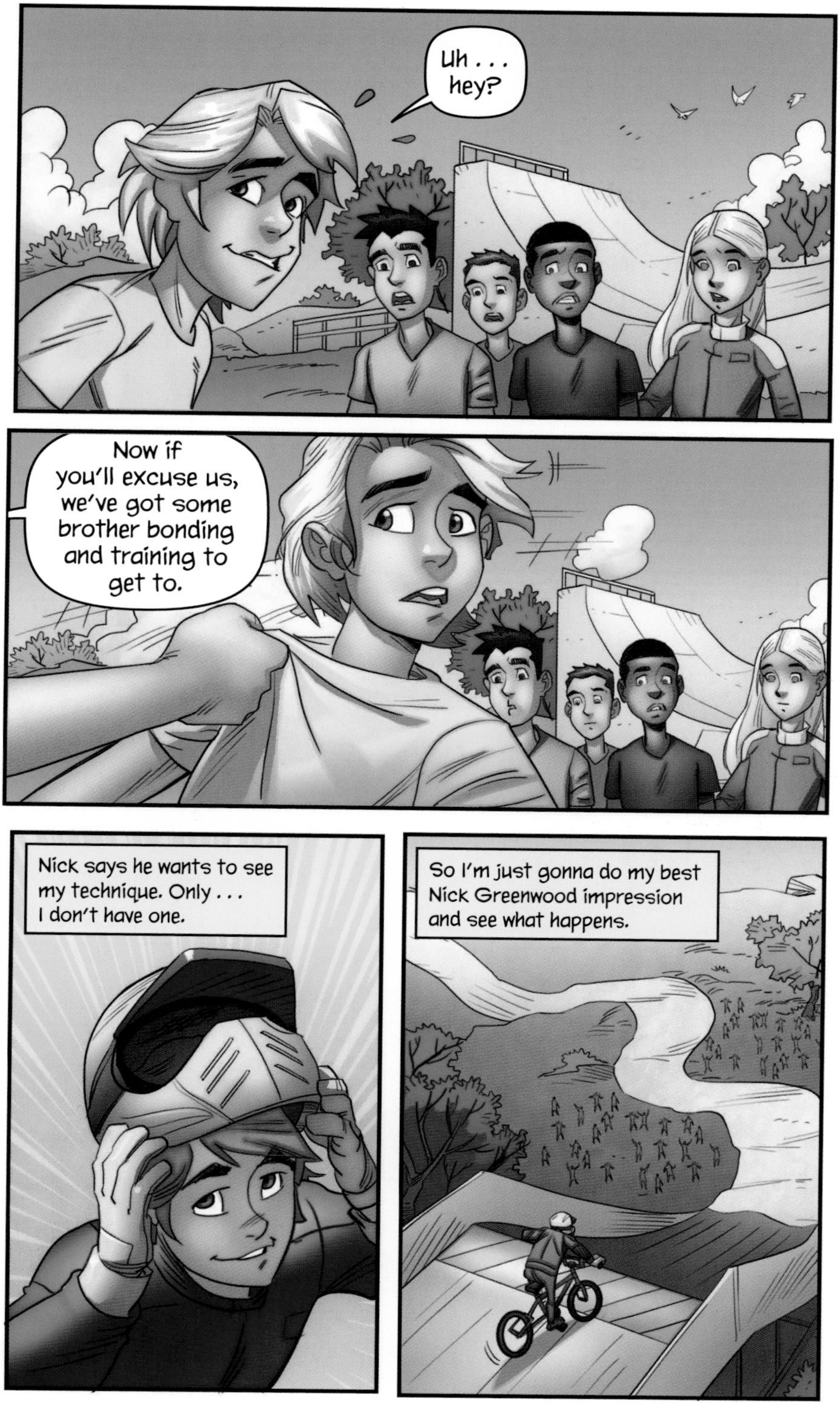
Uh . . . hey?
Now if you'll excuse us, we've got some brother bonding and training to get to.
Nick says he wants to see my technique. Only . . . I don't have one.
So I'm just gonna do my best Nick Greenwood impression and see what happens.

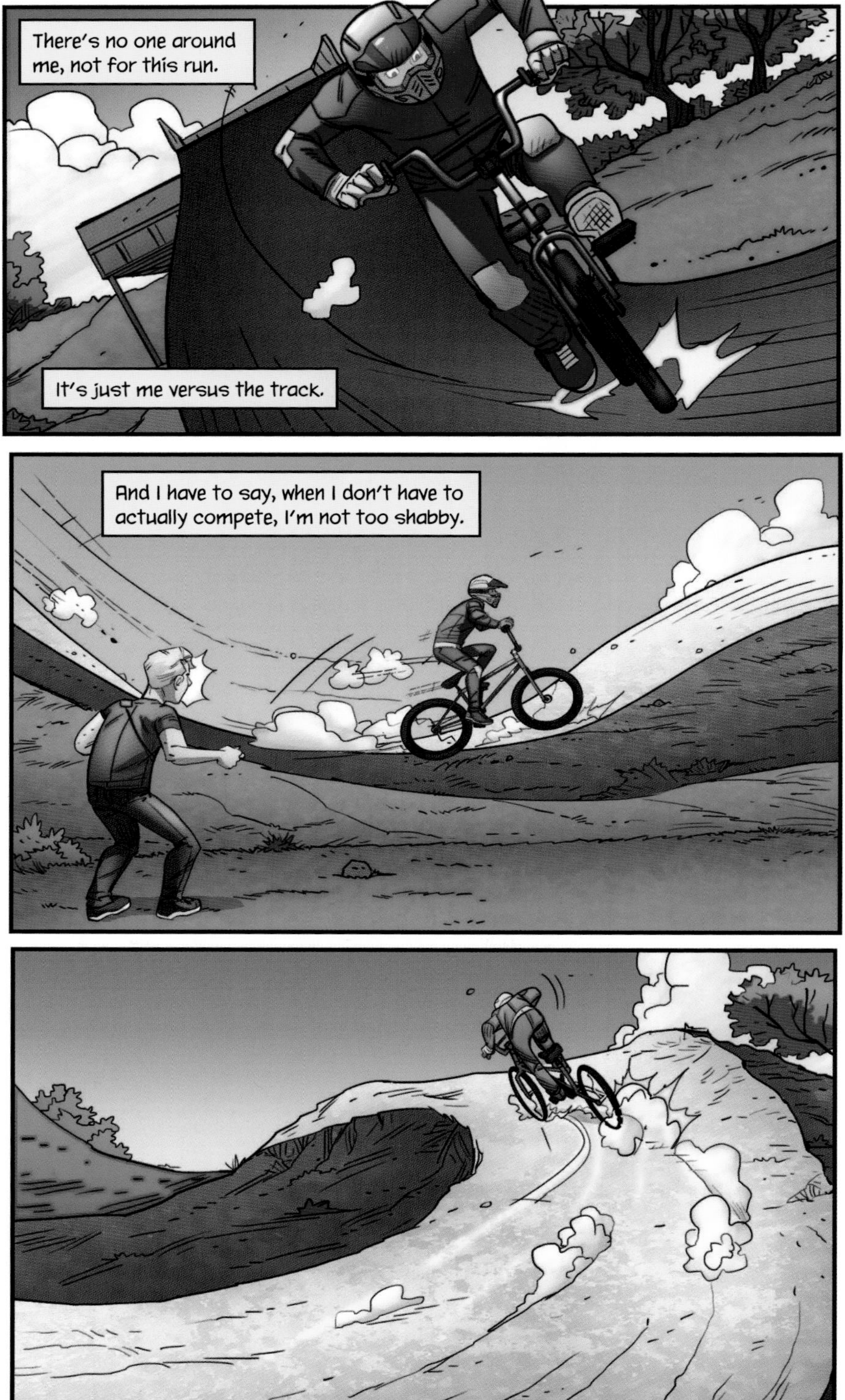
There's no one around me, not for this run.
It's just me versus the track.
And I have to say, when I don't have to actually compete, I'm not too shabby.

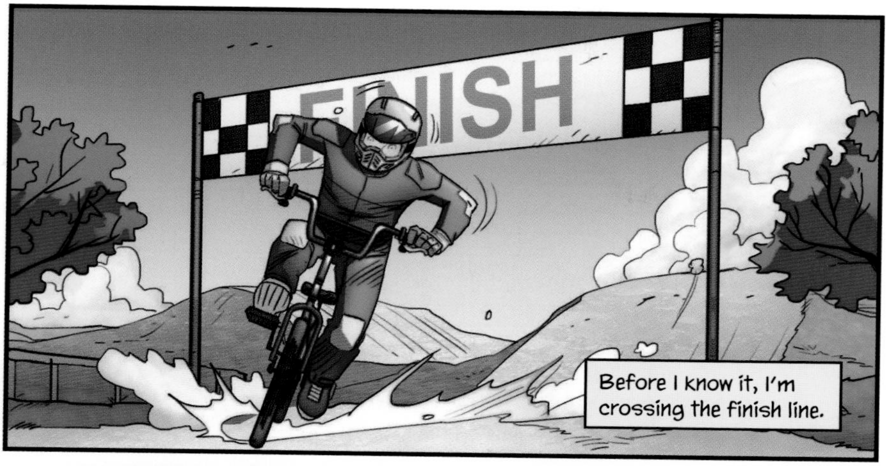
FINISH
Before I know it, I'm crossing the finish line.

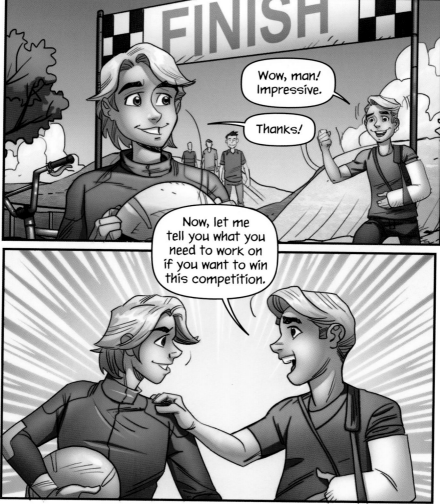

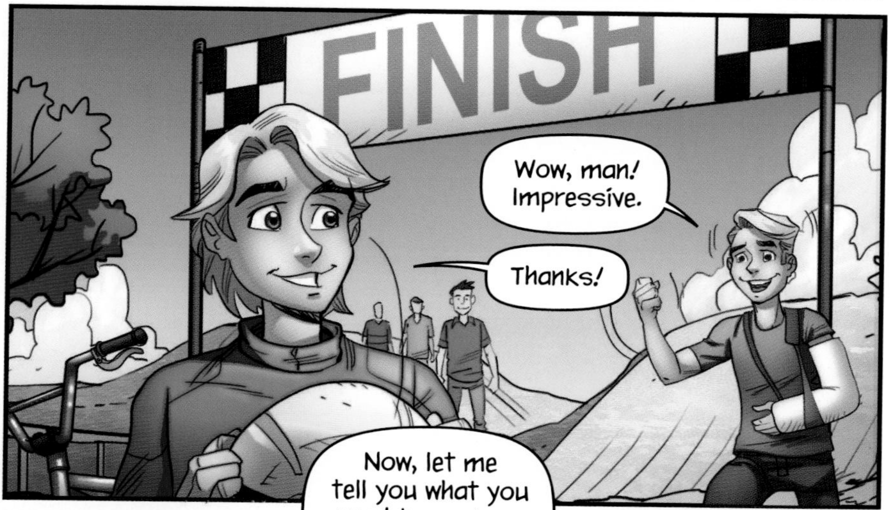
FINISH
Wow, man! Impressive.
Thanks!

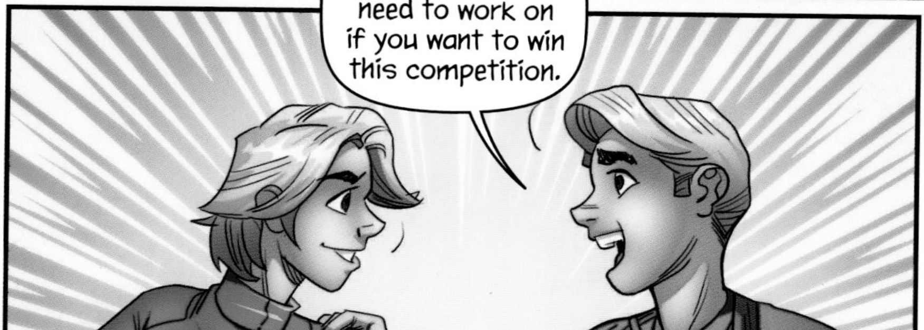
Now, let me tell you what you need to work on if you want to win this competition.

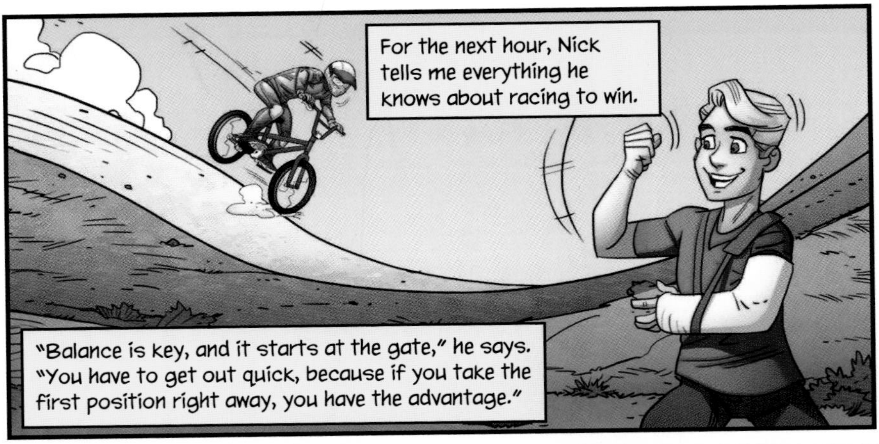
For the next hour, Nick tells me everything he knows about racing to win.
"Balance is key, and it starts at the gate," he says. "You have to get out quick, because if you take the first position right away, you have the advantage."

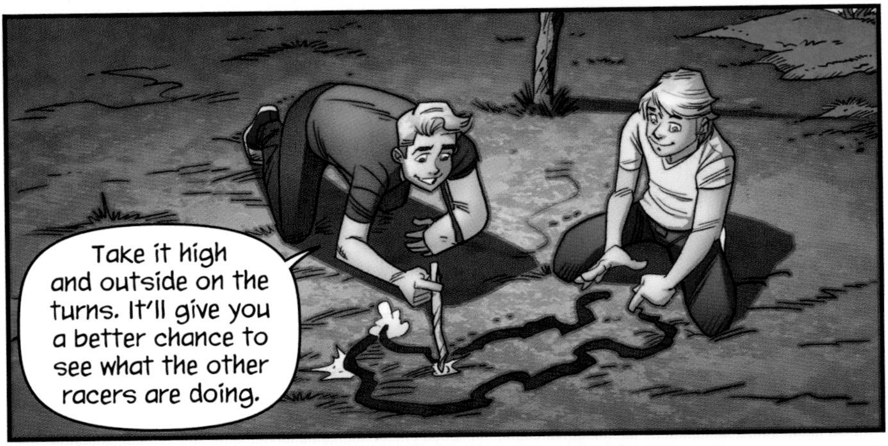
Take it high and outside on the turns. It'll give you a better chance to see what the other racers are doing.

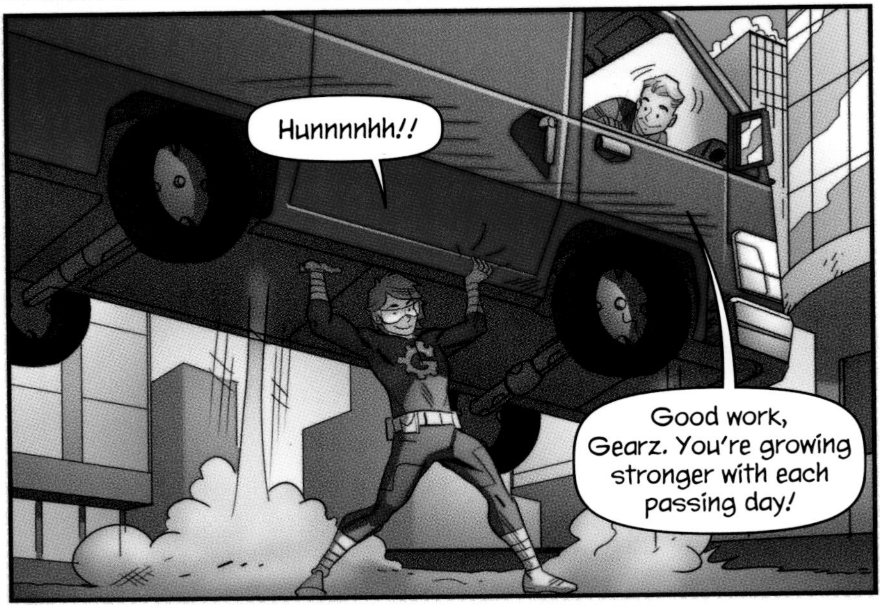
Hunnnnhh!!
Good work, Gearz. You're growing stronger with each passing day!

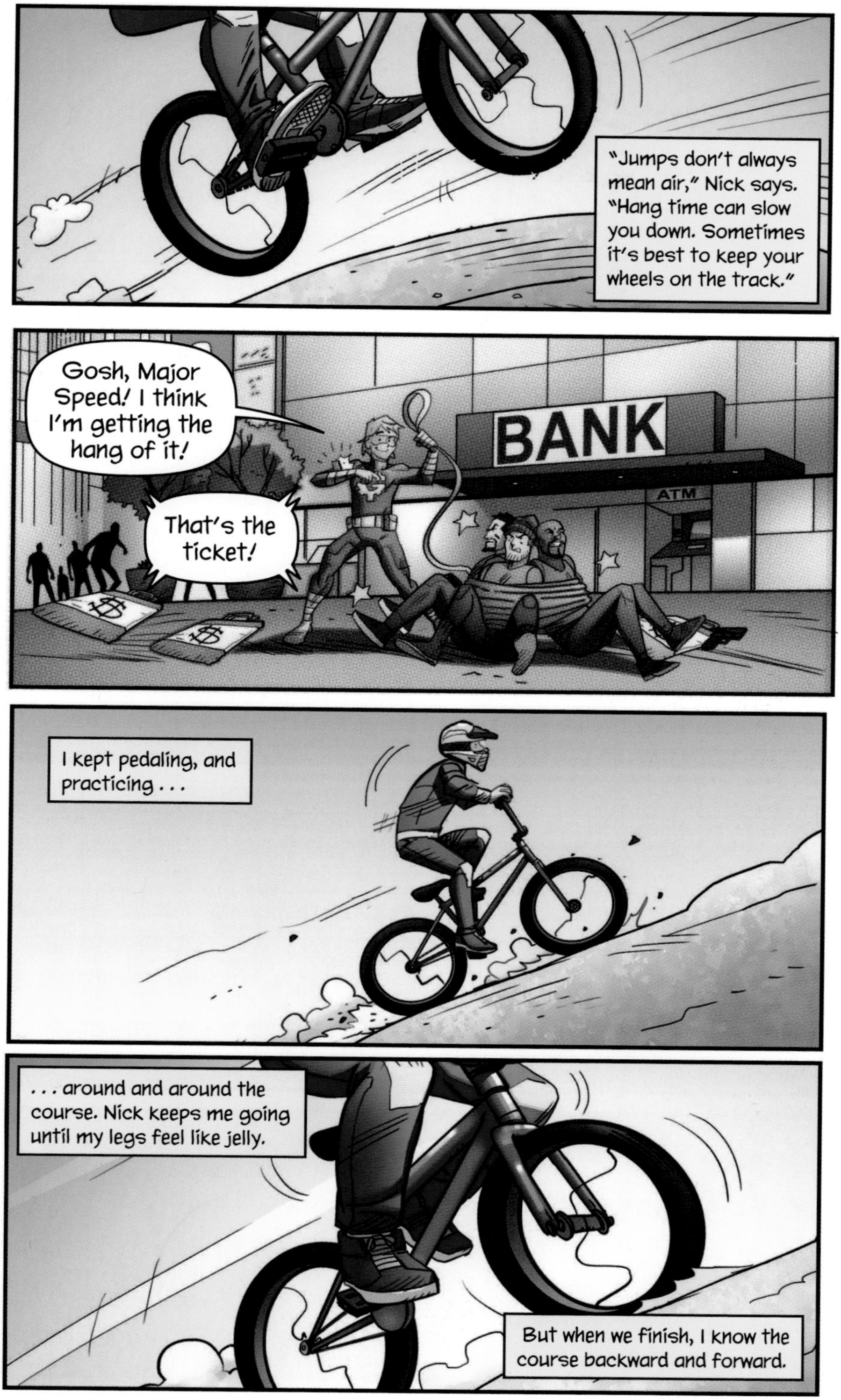
"Jumps don't always mean air," Nick says. "Hang time can slow you down. Sometimes it's best to keep your wheels on the track."
Gosh, Major Speed! I think I'm getting the hang of it!
That's the ticket!
BANK
ATM
I kept pedaling, and practicing . . .
. . . around and around the course. Nick keeps me going until my legs feel like jelly.
But when we finish, I know the course backward and forward.

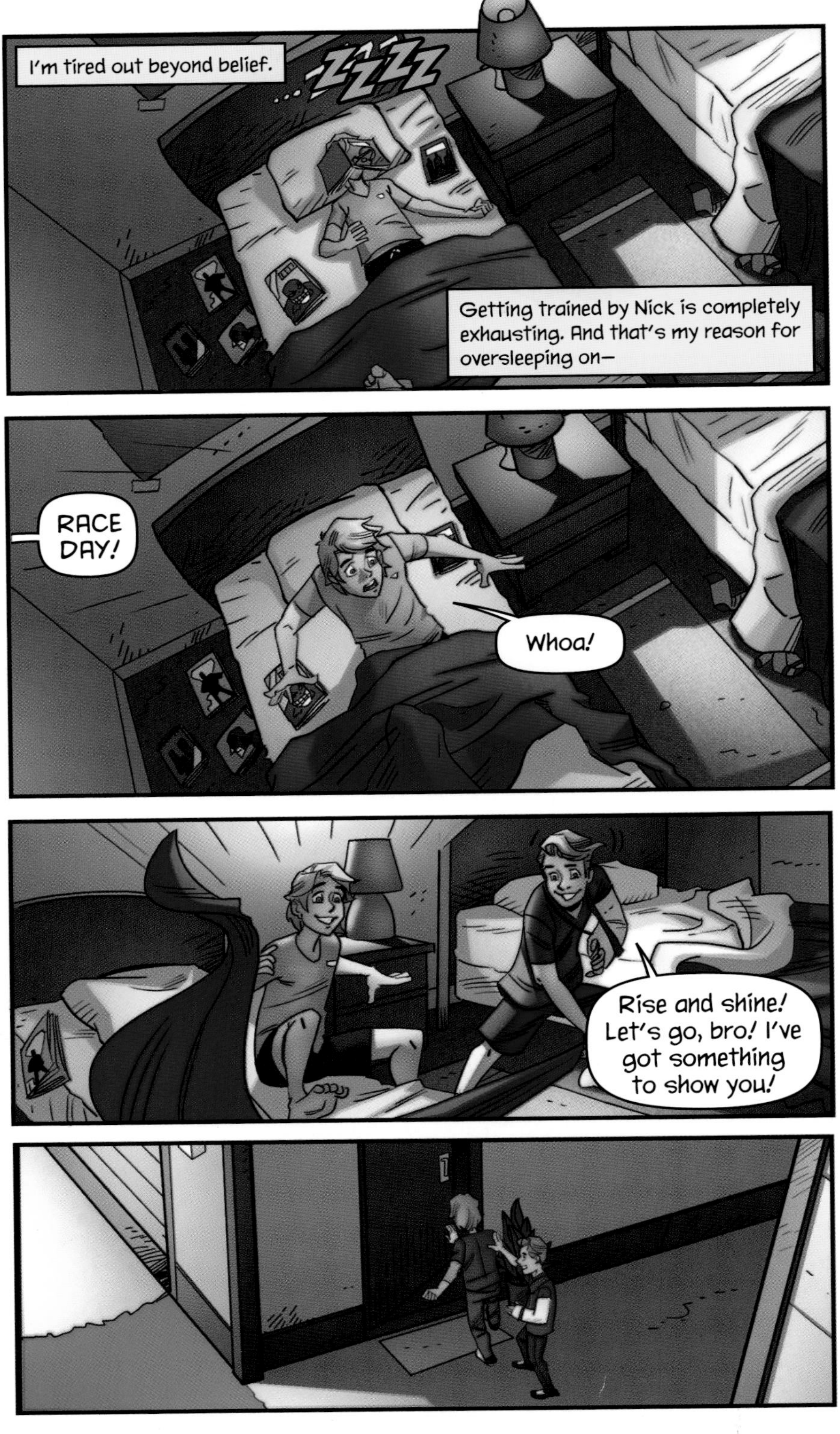
I'm tired out beyond belief.
...ZZZZ
Getting trained by Nick is completely exhausting. And that's my reason for oversleeping on—
RACE DAY!
Whoa!
Rise and shine! Let's go, bro! I've got something to show you!

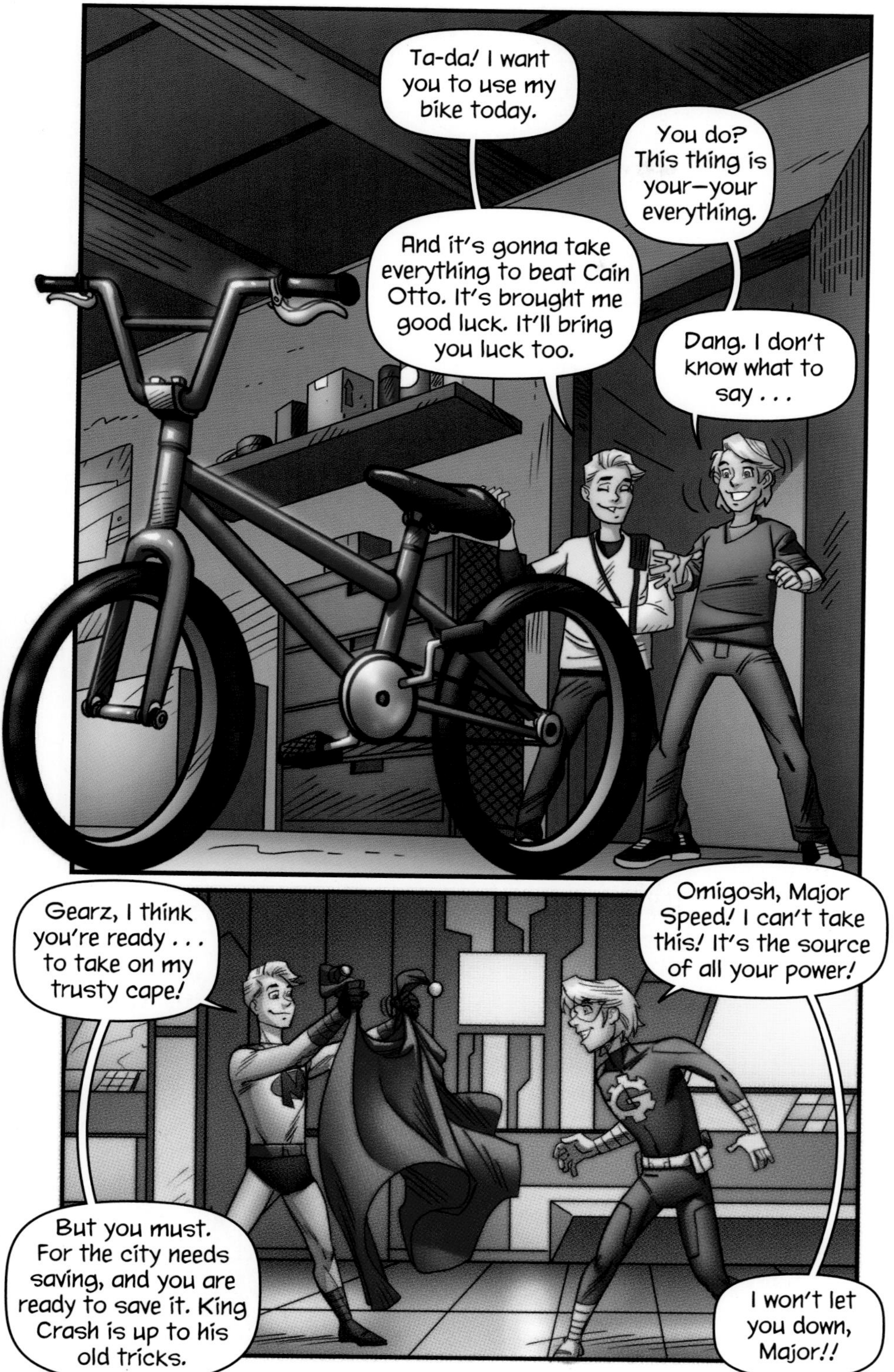

Ta-da! I want you to use my bike today.
You do? This thing is your—your everything.
And it's gonna take everything to beat Cain Otto. It's brought me good luck. It'll bring you luck too.
Dang. I don't know what to say . . .
Gearz, I think you're ready . . . to take on my trusty cape!
Omigosh, Major Speed! I can't take this! It's the source of all your power!
But you must. For the city needs saving, and you are ready to save it. King Crash is up to his old tricks.
I won't let you down, Major!!

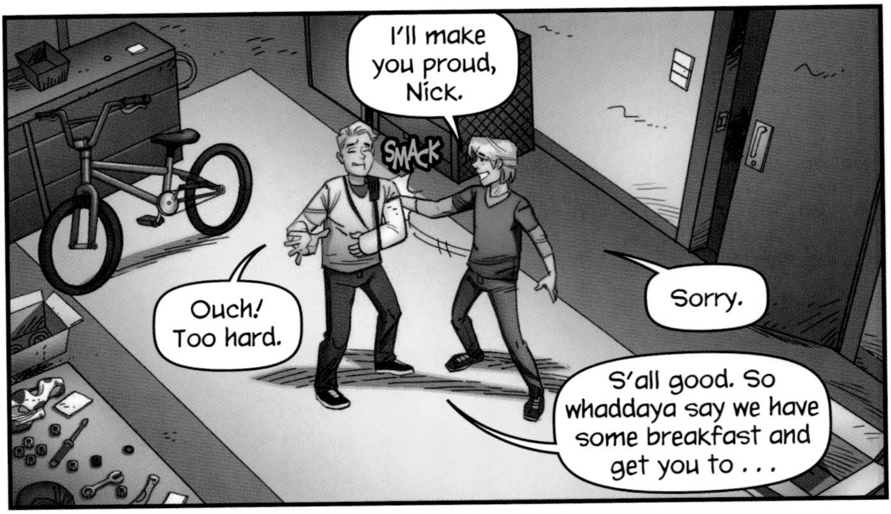
I'll make you proud, Nick.
SMACK
Ouch! Too hard.
Sorry.
S'all good. So whaddaya say we have some breakfast and get you to . . .

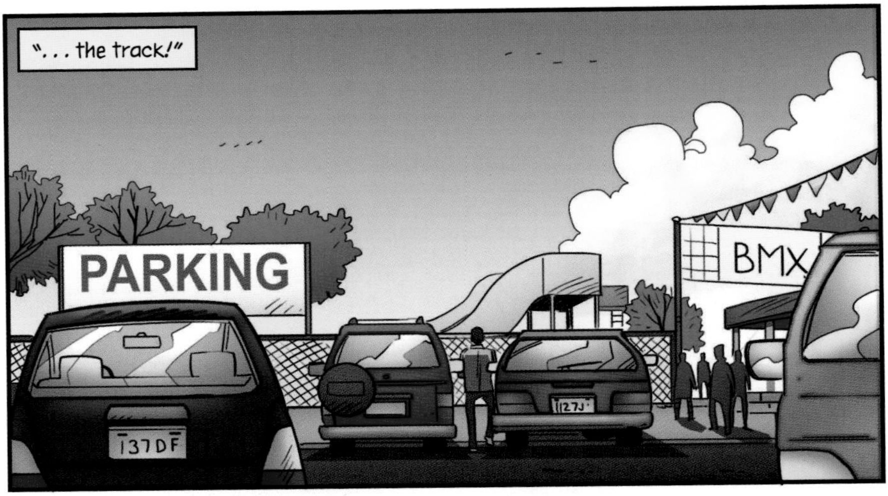
". . . the track!"
PARKING
BMX
137DF

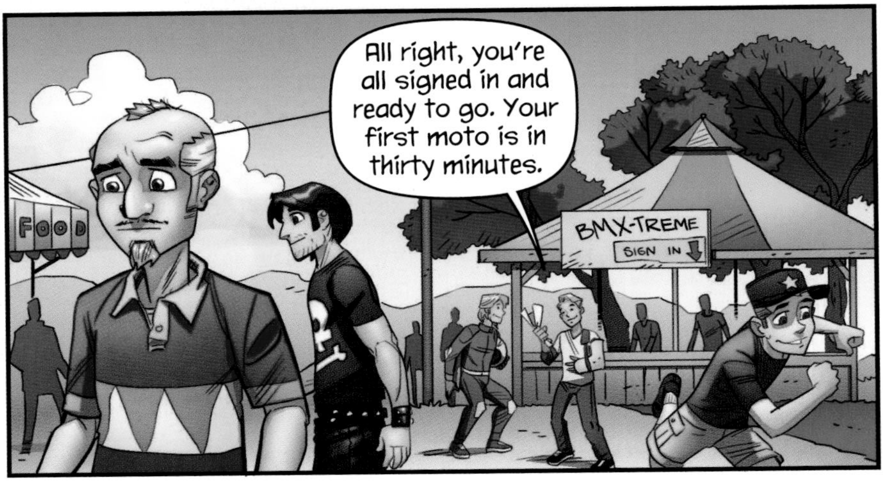
All right, you're all signed in and ready to go. Your first moto is in thirty minutes.
FOOD
BMX-TREME
SIGN IN

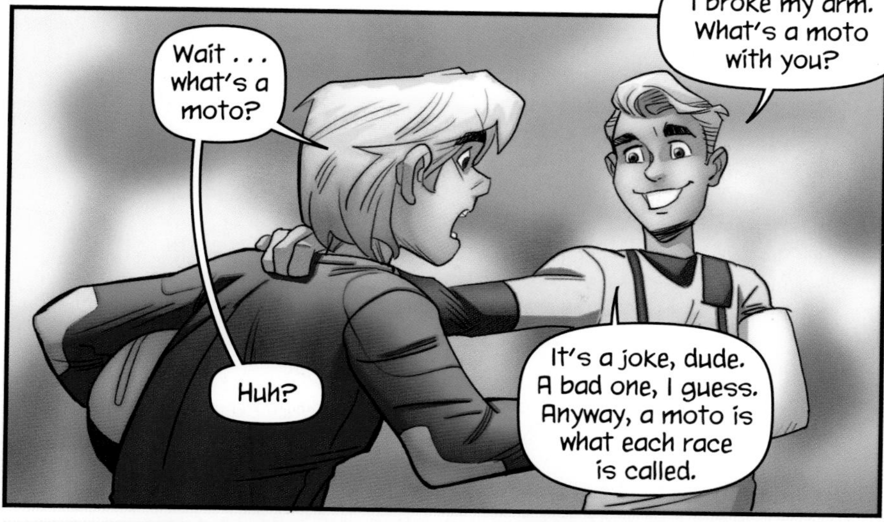
Wait . . . what's a moto?
I broke my arm. What's a moto with you?
Huh?
It's a joke, dude. A bad one, I guess. Anyway, a moto is what each race is called.

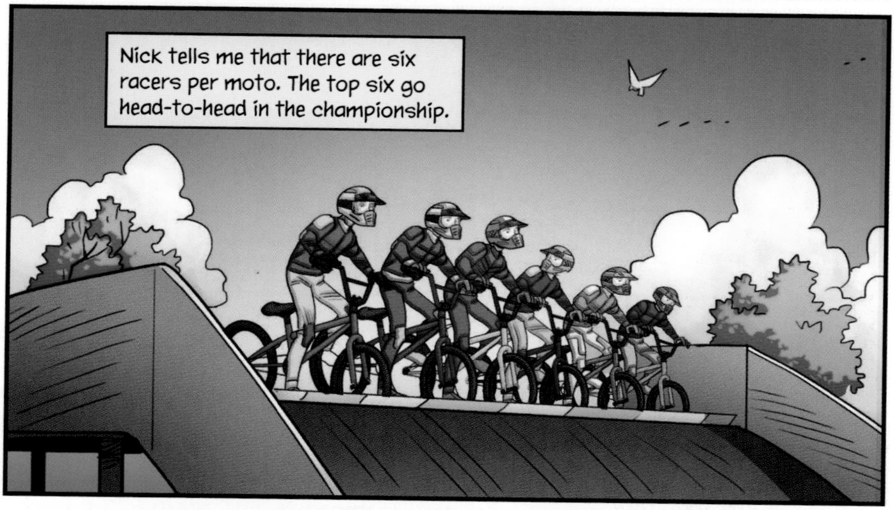
Nick tells me that there are six racers per moto. The top six go head-to-head in the championship.

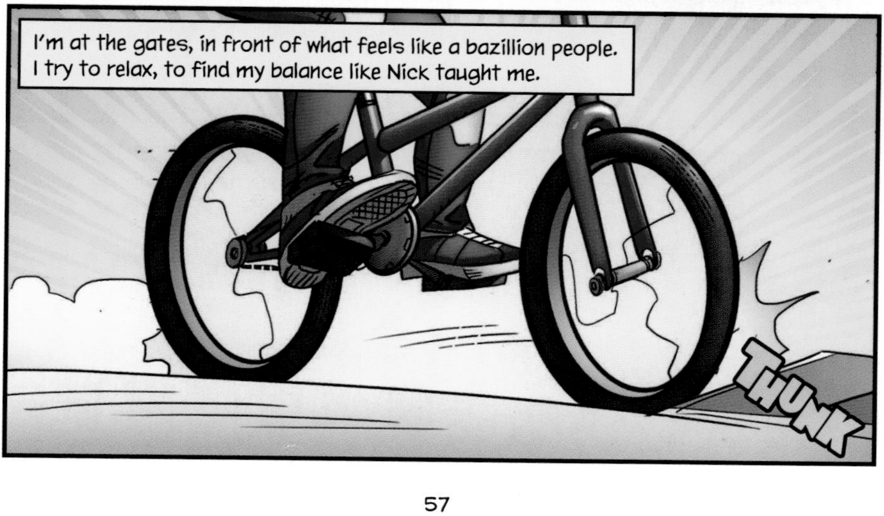
I'm at the gates, in front of what feels like a bazillion people. I try to relax, to find my balance like Nick taught me.
THUNK

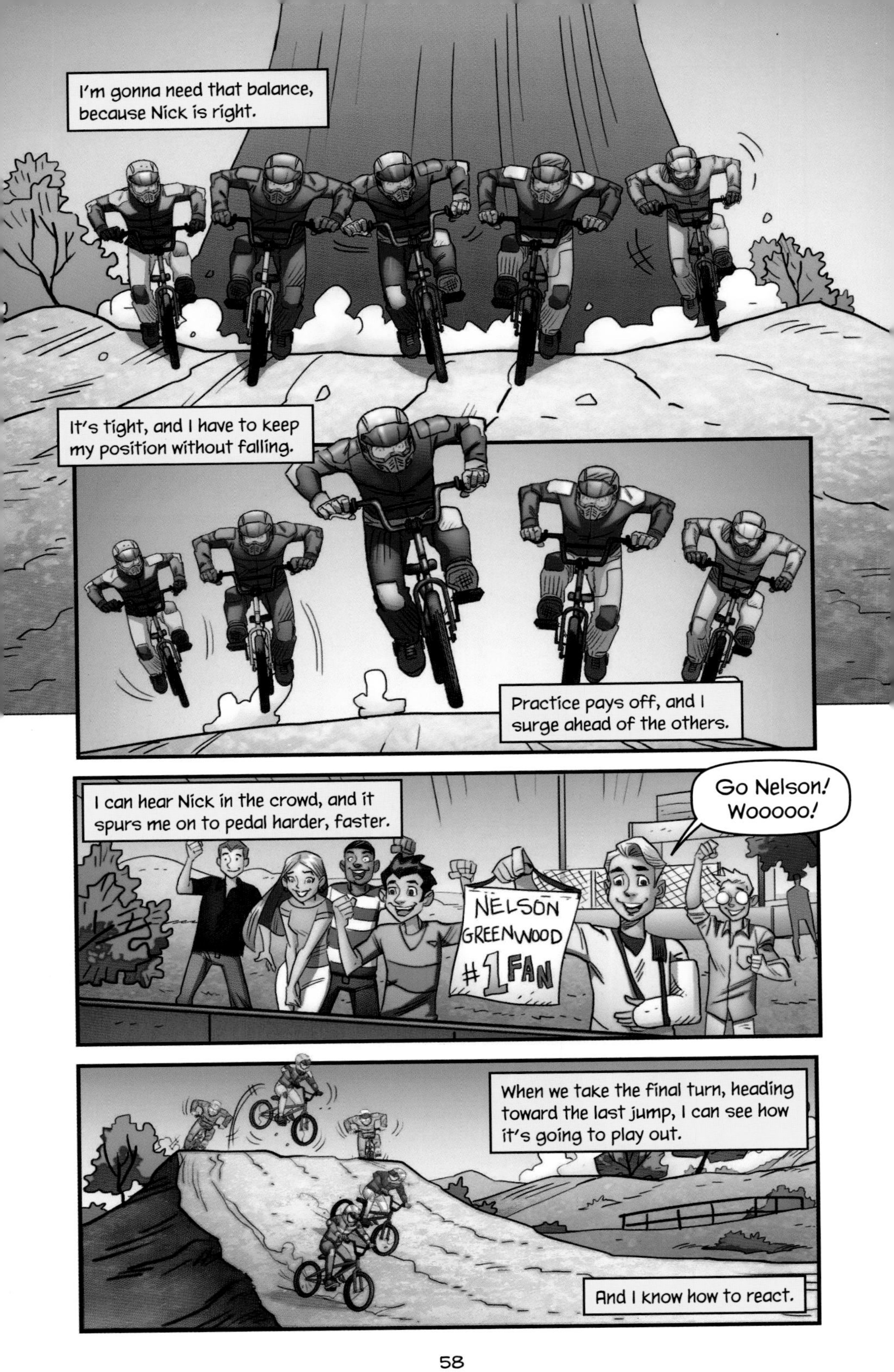
I'm gonna need that balance, because Nick is right.
It's tight, and I have to keep my position without falling.
Practice pays off, and I surge ahead of the others.
I can hear Nick in the crowd, and it spurs me on to pedal harder, faster.
Go Nelson! Wooooo!
NELSON GREENWOOD #1 FAN
When we take the final turn, heading toward the last jump, I can see how it's going to play out.
And I know how to react.

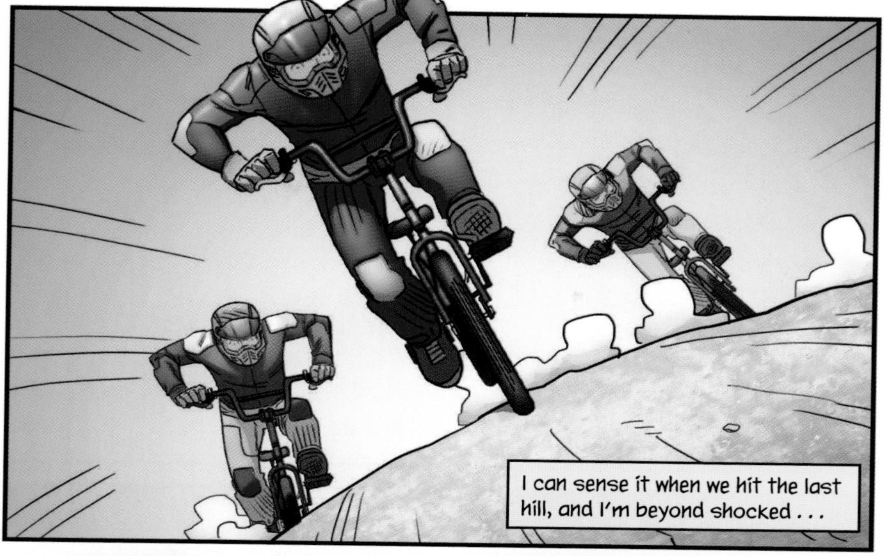
I can sense it when we hit the last hill, and I'm beyond shocked . . .

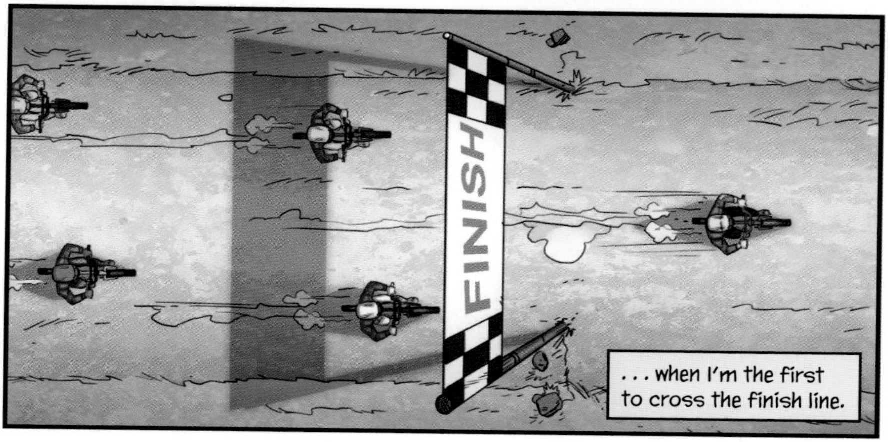
FINISH
. . . when I'm the first to cross the finish line.

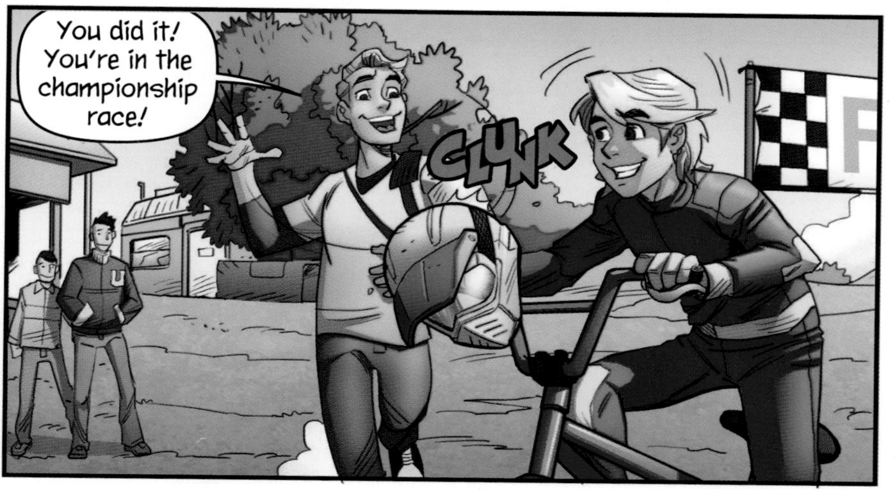
You did it! You're in the championship race!
CLUNK

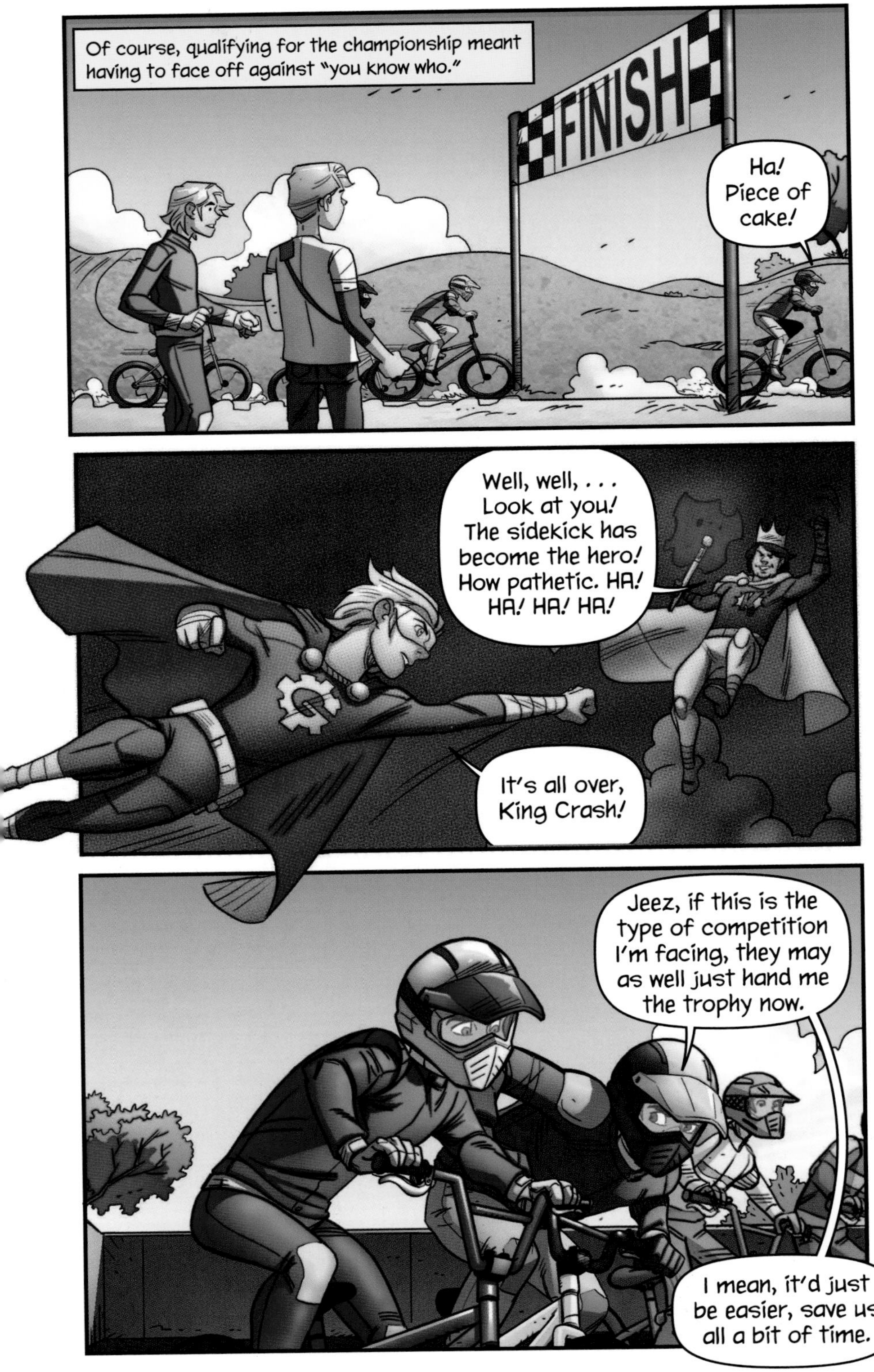
Of course, qualifying for the championship meant having to face off against "you know who."
FINISH
Ha! Piece of cake!
Well, well, . . . Look at you! The sidekick has become the hero! How pathetic. HA! HA! HA! HA!
It's all over, King Crash!
Jeez, if this is the type of competition I'm facing, they may as well just hand me the trophy now.
I mean, it'd just be easier, save us all a bit of time.

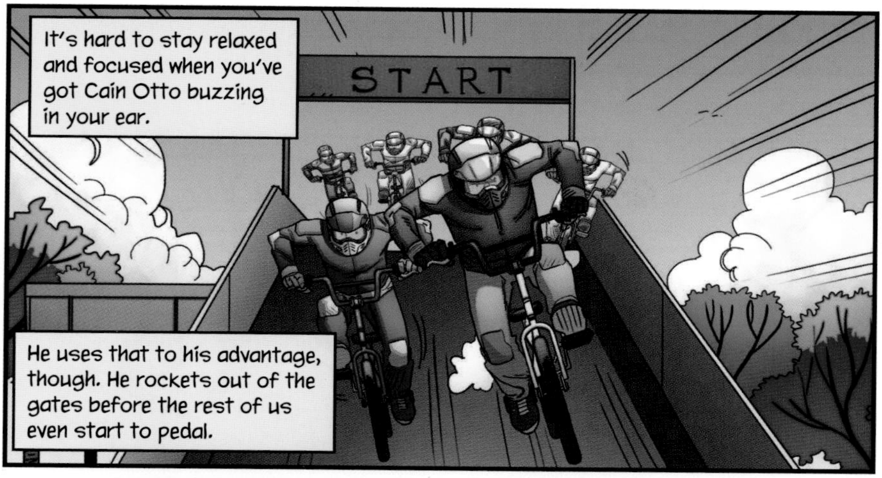
It's hard to stay relaxed and focused when you've got Cain Otto buzzing in your ear.
START
He uses that to his advantage, though. He rockets out of the gates before the rest of us even start to pedal.

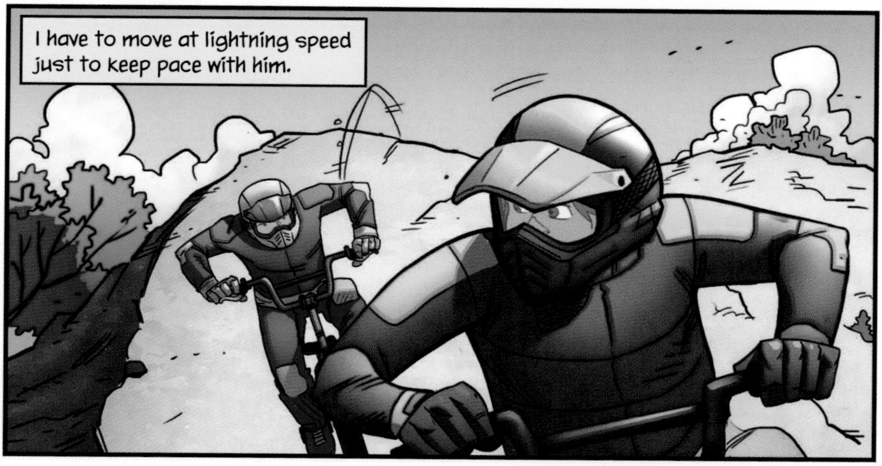
I have to move at lightning speed just to keep pace with him.

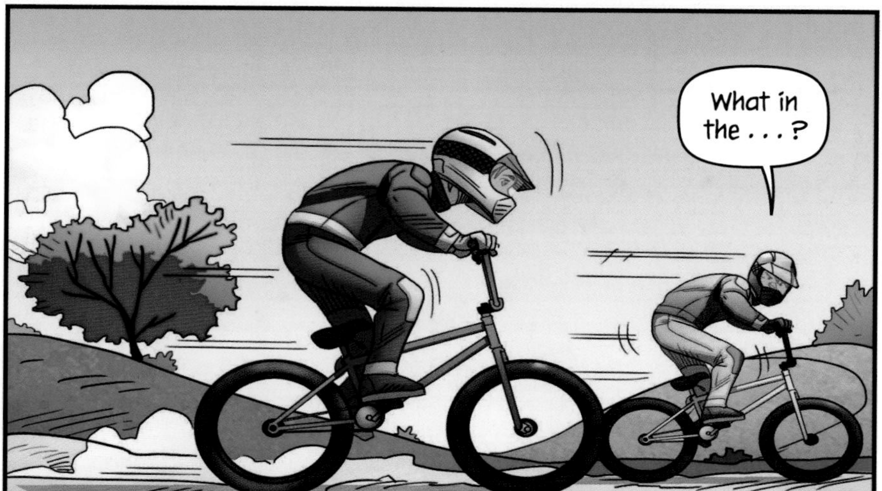
What in the . . . ?

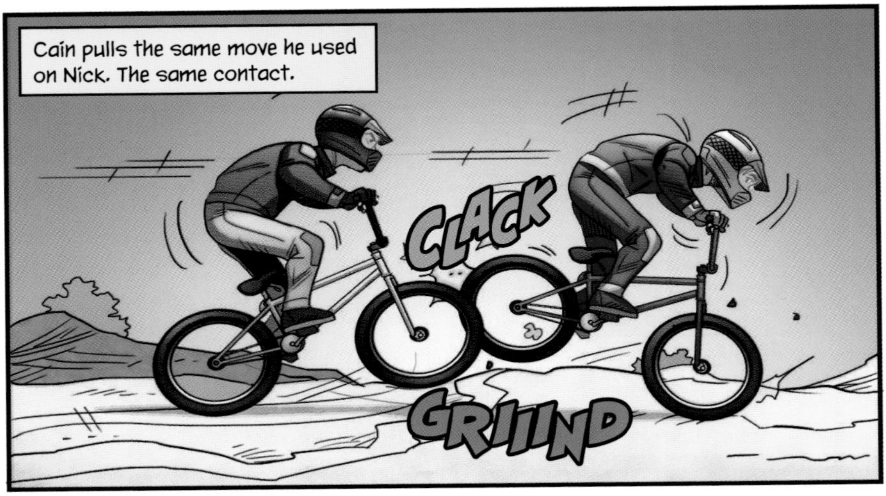
Cain pulls the same move he used on Nick. The same contact.
CLACK
GRIIIND

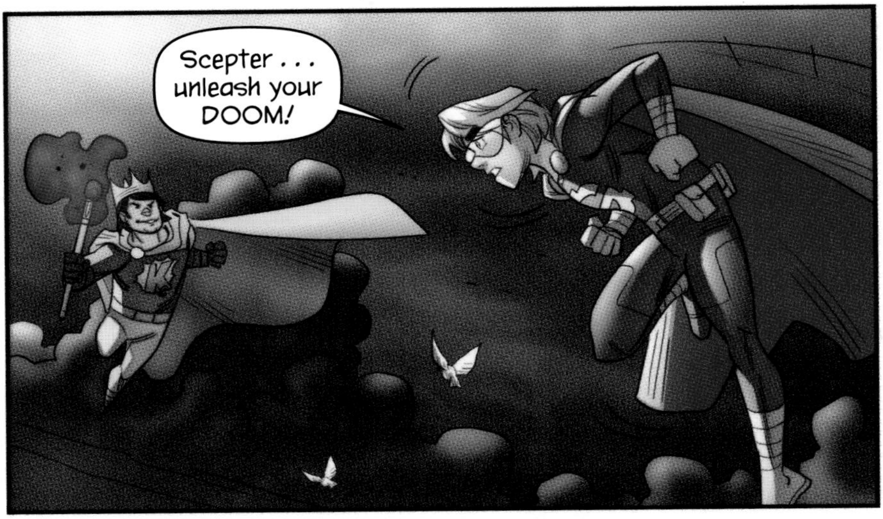
Scepter . . . unleash your DOOM!

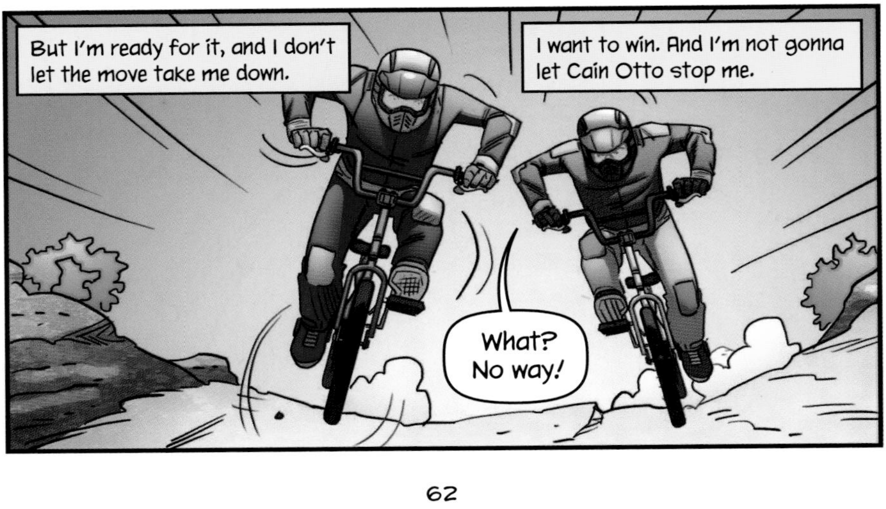
But I'm ready for it, and I don't let the move take me down.
I want to win. And I'm not gonna let Cain Otto stop me.
What? No way!

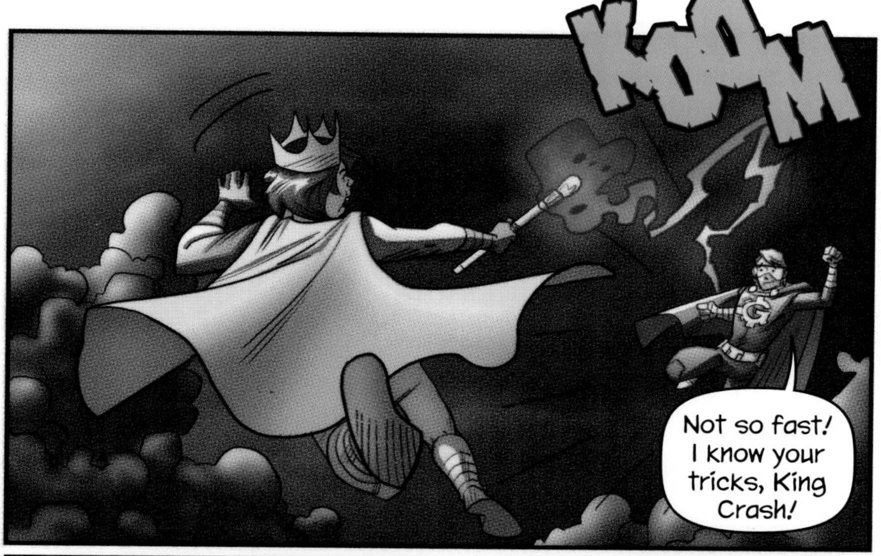
KOOM
Not so fast! I know your tricks, King Crash!

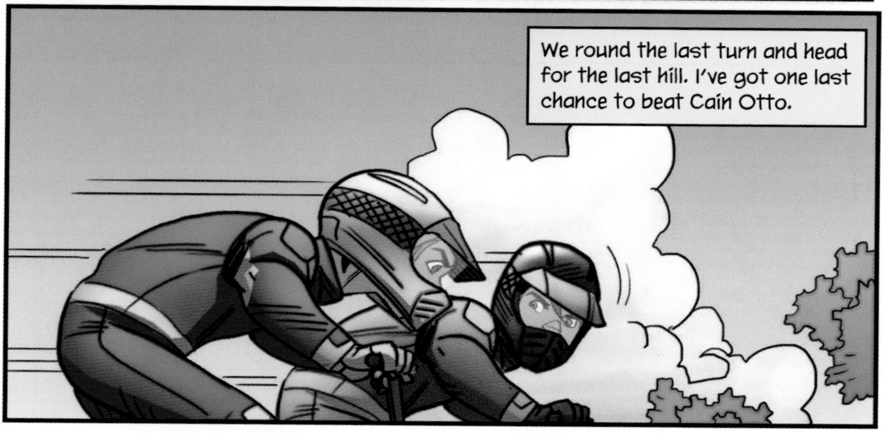
We round the last turn and head for the last hill. I've got one last chance to beat Cain Otto.

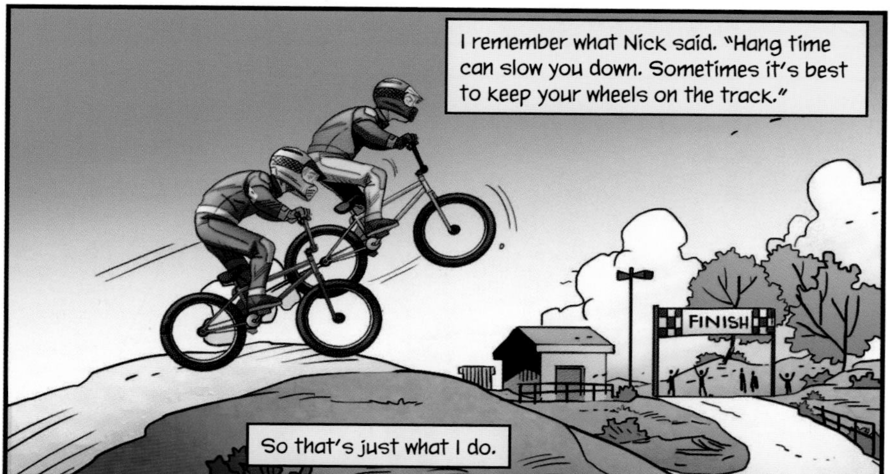
I remember what Nick said. "Hang time can slow you down. Sometimes it's best to keep your wheels on the track."
FINISH
So that's just what I do.

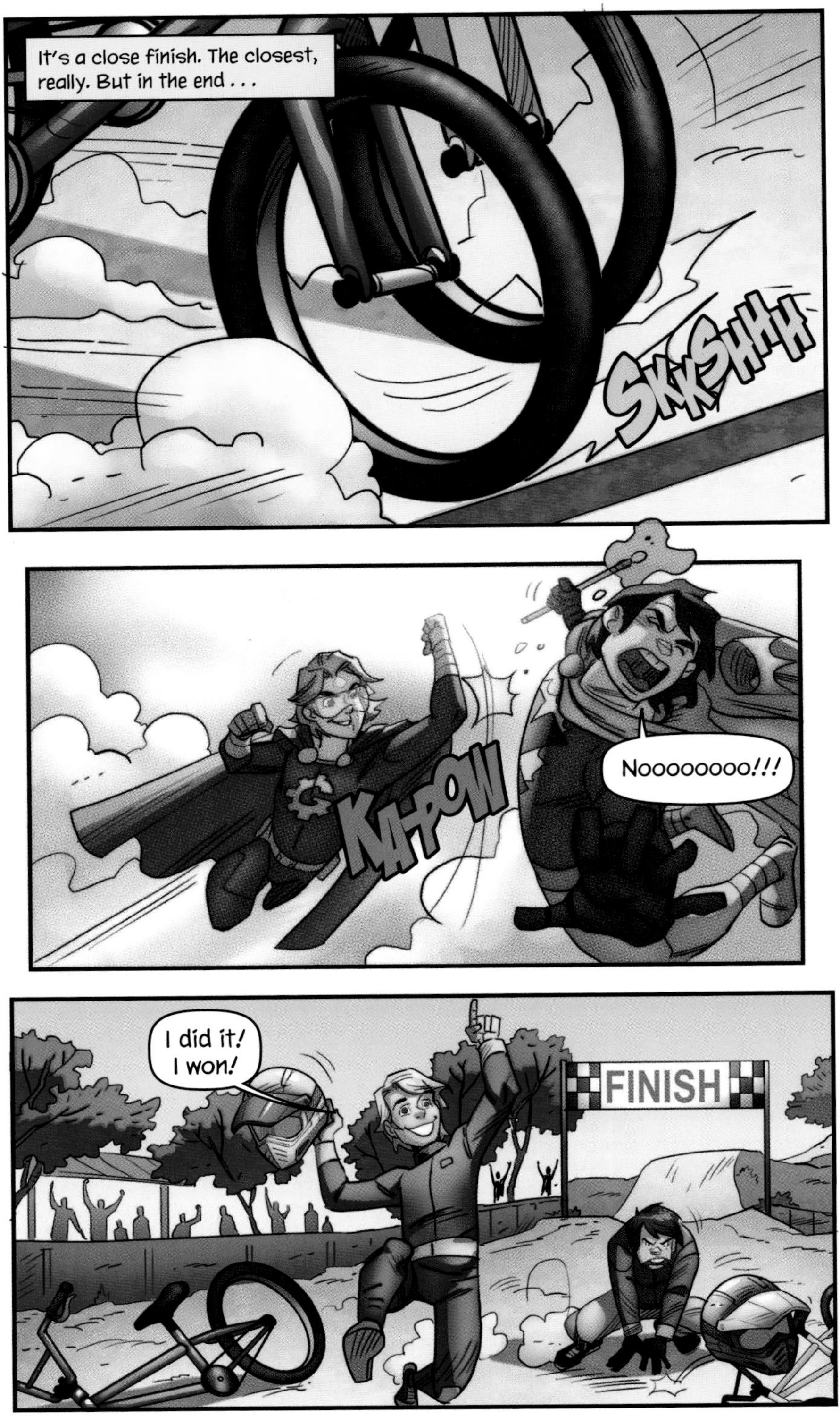
It's a close finish. The closest, really. But in the end . . .
SKKSHHH
KA-POW
Noooooooo!!!
I did it! I won!
FINISH

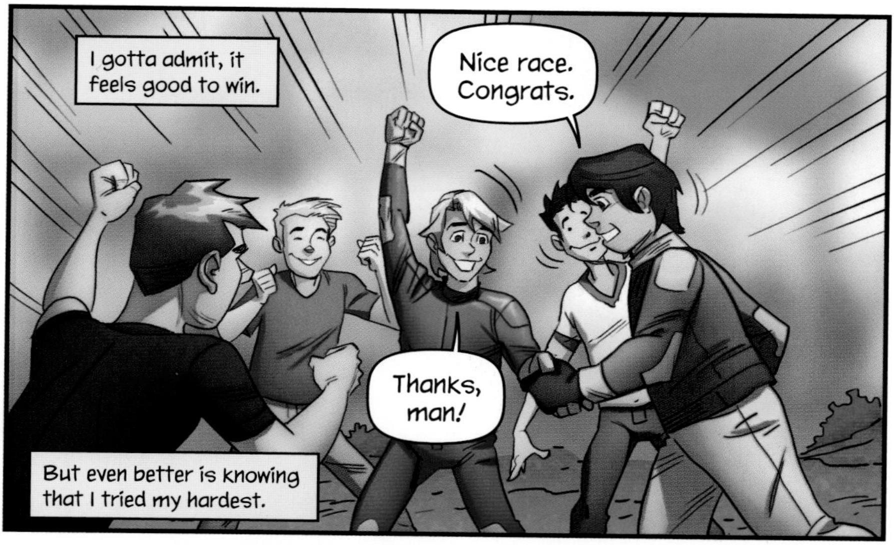
I gotta admit, it feels good to win.
Nice race. Congrats.
Thanks, man!
But even better is knowing that I tried my hardest.

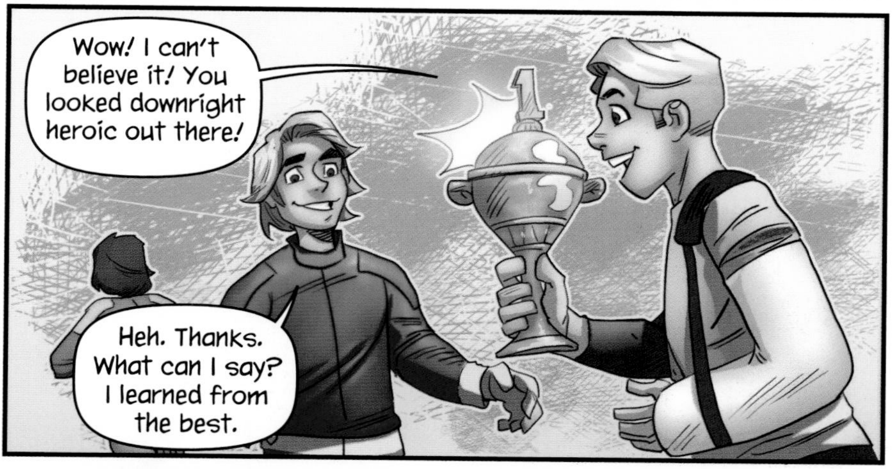
Wow! I can't believe it! You looked downright heroic out there!
Heh. Thanks. What can I say? I learned from the best.

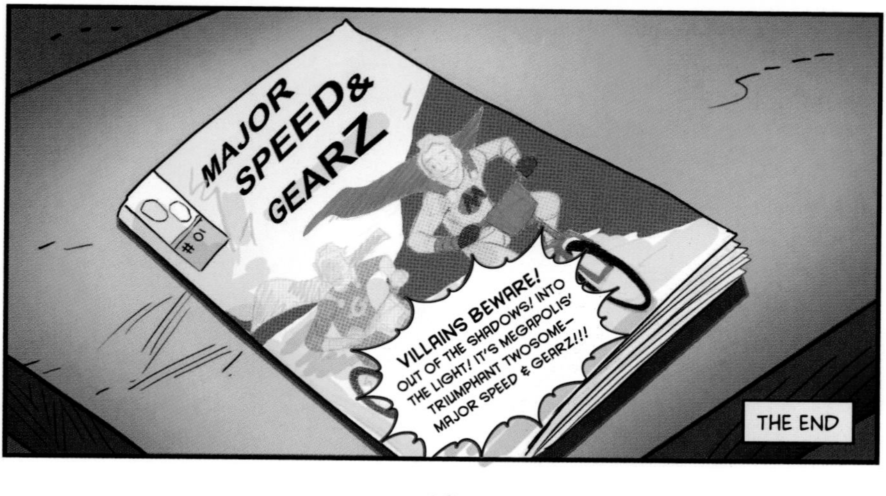
MAJOR SPEED & GEARZ
#01
VILLAINS BEWARE! OUT OF THE SHADOWS! INTO THE LIGHT! IT'S MEGAPOLIS' TRIUMPHANT TWOSOME— MAJOR SPEED & GEARZ!!!
THE END

VISUAL QUESTIONS

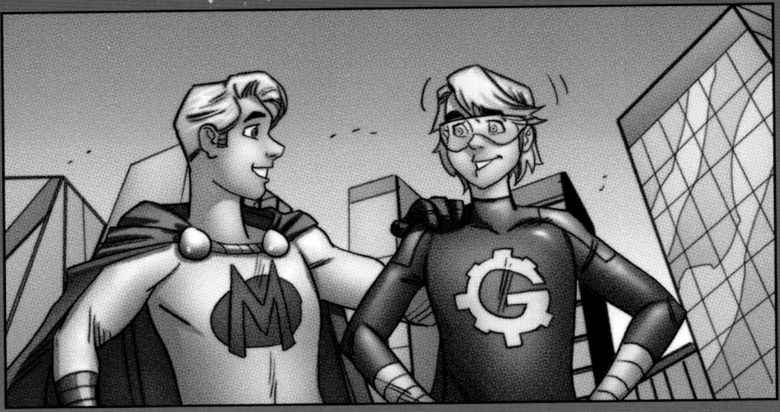
M
G

1. The characters in Nelson's comic book, Major Speed and Gearz, strongly resemble himself and his twin brother Nick. From the above panel, how do you think Nelson feels about his relationship to his brother? Explain your answer.

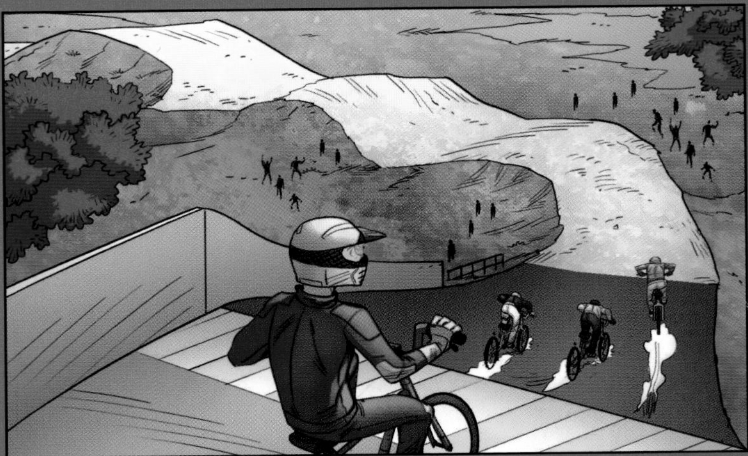

2. Graphic artists often use dramatic angles to help show what a character is feeling. Look at the above panel. What do you think Nelson is thinking or feeling in this scene?

3. Graphic art can often show what's happening in a scene without needing any words. Look at the panels to the right. Describe what you think is happening. What has changed between the panels, and why has the change occurred?

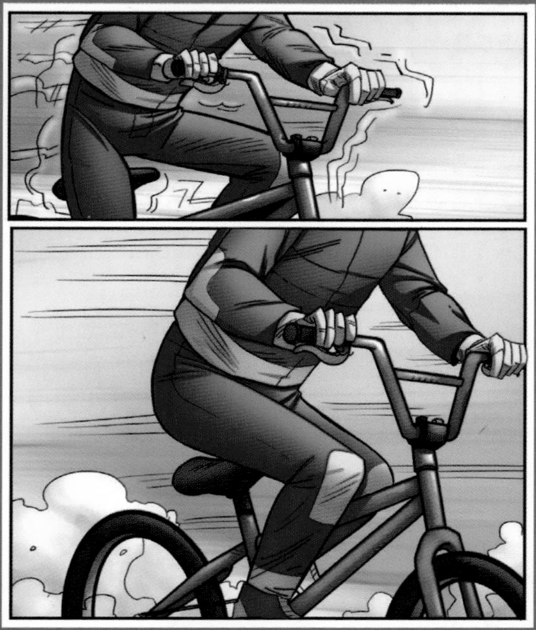

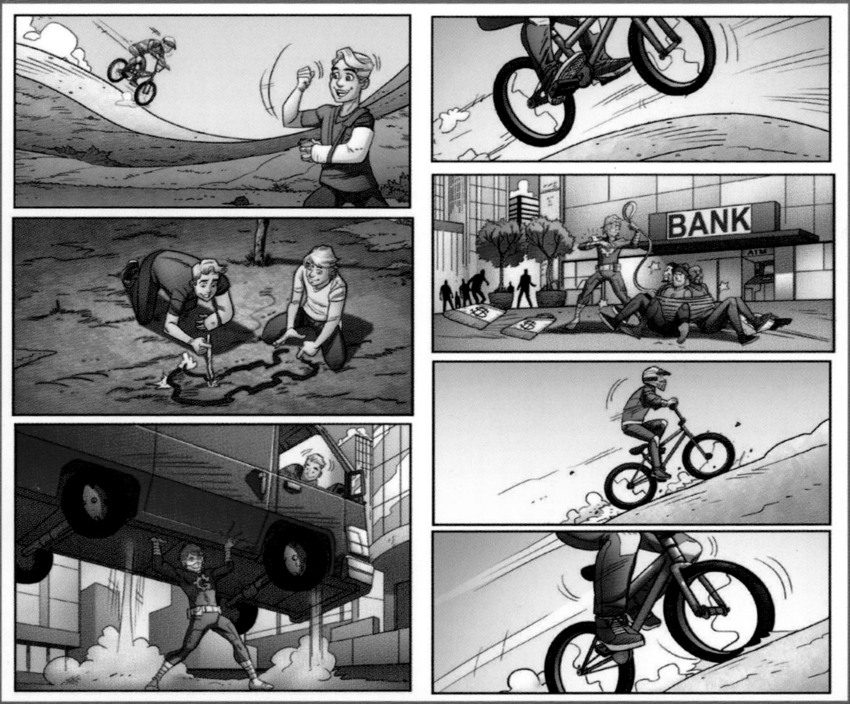
BANK
ATM

4. Sometimes a series of panels is used to show the passage of time in the story. Look at the series of panels above. Can you describe how Nelson's character grows and changes based on what the panels show?

MORE ABOUT BMX

- BMX is a cycling sport made up of extreme, motocross-style racing on tracks with incline starts and several obstacles on the course. BMX stands for Bicycle Moto Cross.

- BMX was invented in the late 1960s in Southern California. It was created because of the popularity of motocross, or off-road motorcycle racing.

- A standard BMX bike is smaller than an average road bike and has a fixed frame. It also has only one gear, which makes racing easier. There are three specific bike models: traditional, freestyle, and jump.

- An average BMX race lasts about 25 to 40 seconds, and racers reach speeds up to 35 miles (56 kilometers) per hour!

- Dirt racetracks usually measure about 1,000 feet (305 meters) in length.

- BMX is also an Olympic sport. It became a medal sport in the 2008 Summer Games in Beijing, China.

- Today, freestyle BMX is a major event at the Summer X Games.

AWESOME BMX MOVES

BARSPIN — To complete a barspin, hop your BMX into the air. Throw your handlebars so they spin while you're in mid-jump, and catch them before you land.

BUNNY-HOP — A bunny-hop is when both the front and back wheels of your BMX jump off the ground at the same time. It's used to jump over small obstacles.

FLATSPIN — While in the air during a high jump, do a complete horizontal spin on your BMX before landing.

FRONT POGO — A 'pogo' can be done on either your front or back wheel. For a front pogo, apply your front and rear brakes until the back wheel comes off the ground. Then hop on the front wheel like you would on a pogo stick.

MANUAL — A manual is basically riding your BMX on the back wheel, with the front wheel up in the air for a long period of time. Use your arms and legs to maintain your balance.

TAIL WHIP — To perform a tail whip, catch air and rotate your BMX frame once around the handlebars, which remain stationary.

X-UP — After going off a jump, spin your BMX's handlebars 180 degrees, so that your arms form the letter X. Quickly rotate them back before landing.

GLOSSARY

advantage (ad-VAN-tij)—something that helps you or is useful to you, especially in a competition

archenemy (AHRCH-en-uh-mee)—a chief or main enemy of someone, usually of a superhero character

concession stand (kuhn-SESH-uhn STAND)—a booth where people can buy food and drink

confidence (KON-fuh-duhnss)—the trust one has in a person or thing

confound (kon-FOUND)—to perplex or confuse, especially by a sudden display or surprise

deja vu (DEY-zhah VOO)—a feeling of having experienced something before

devious (DEE-vee-uhss)—tricky or clever

gallant (GAL-uhnt)—brave and fearless

grotesque (groh-TESK)—very strange or ugly

nefarious (ni-FAIR-ee-uhs)—extremely wicked or villainous

phenomenal (fuh-NOM-uh-nuhl)—amazing or astonishing

sidekick (SAYHD-kik)—a close friend and assistant to a superhero

technique (tek-NEEK)—a method or way of doing something that requires skill

READ THEM ALL!

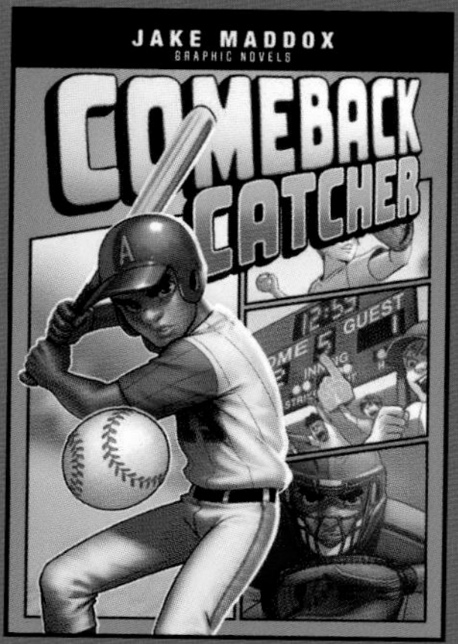
JAKE MADDOX
GRAPHIC NOVELS
COMEBACK CATCHER

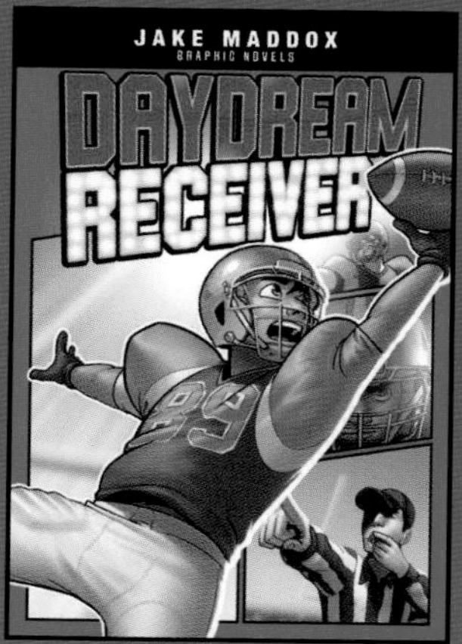
JAKE MADDOX
GRAPHIC NOVELS
DAYDREAM RECEIVER

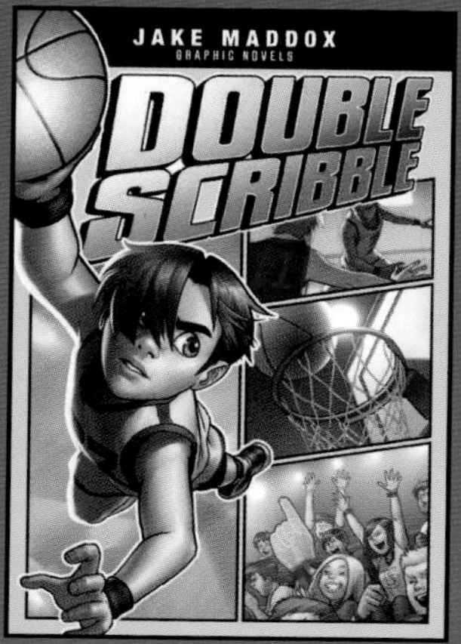
JAKE MADDOX
GRAPHIC NOVELS
DOUBLE SCRIBBLE

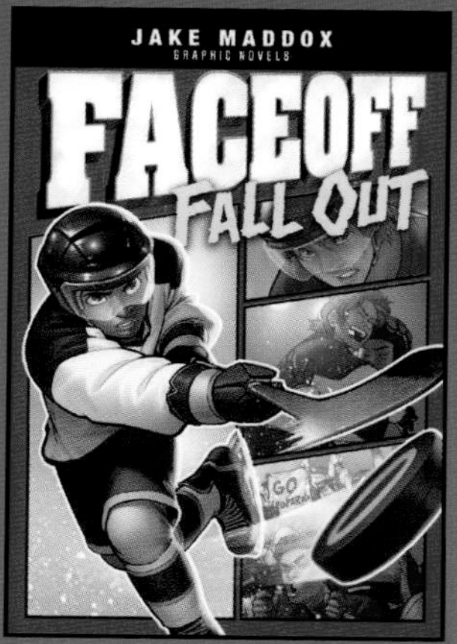
JAKE MADDOX
GRAPHIC NOVELS
FACEOFF FALL OUT

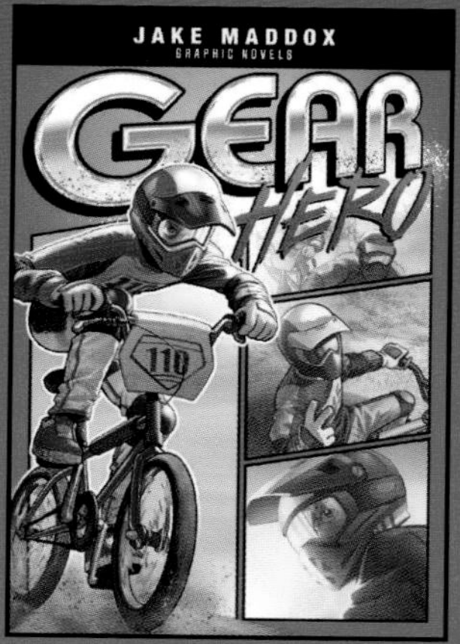
JAKE MADDOX
GRAPHIC NOVELS
GEAR HERO

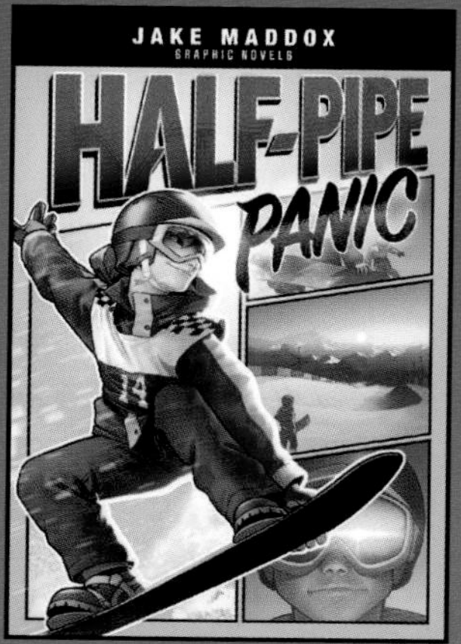
JAKE MADDOX
GRAPHIC NOVELS
HALF-PIPE PANIC

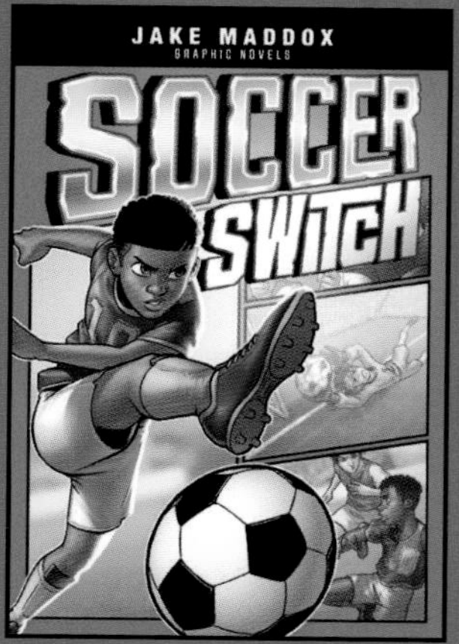
JAKE MADDOX
GRAPHIC NOVELS
SOCCER SWITCH

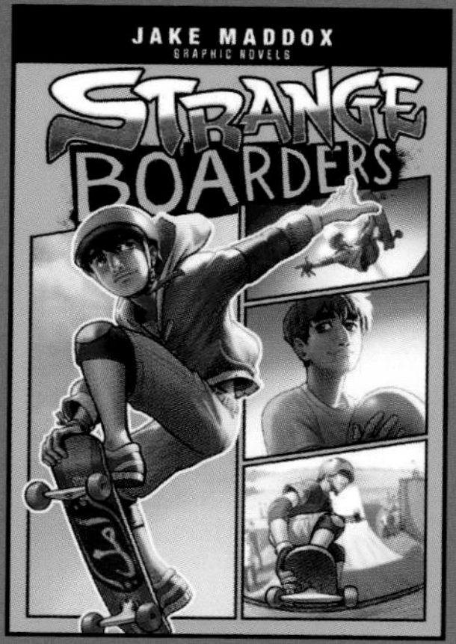
JAKE MADDOX
GRAPHIC NOVELS
STRANGE BOARDERS

ABOUT THE AUTHOR

Brandon Terrell is the author of numerous children's books, including several volumes in both the Tony Hawk 900 Revolution series and the Tony Hawk Live2Skate series. He has also written several Spine Shivers titles, and is the author of the Sports Illustrated Kids: Time Machine Magazine series. When not hunched over his laptop, Brandon enjoys watching movies and TV, reading, watching and playing baseball, and spending time with his wife and two children at his home in Minnesota.

ABOUT THE ARTISTS

Eduardo Garcia works out of Mexico City. He has lent his illustration talents to such varied projects as the Spider-Man Family, Flash Gordon, and Speed Racer. He's currently working on a series of illustrations for an educational publisher while his wife and children look over his shoulder!

Benny Fuentes is a Mexican-based digital illustrator who has worked on several books for companies such as Marvel, DC, Image Comics, and of course, Capstone Publishers. He also works as a volunteer at a local animal shelter during his free time.

Jaymes Reed has operated the company Digital-CAPS: Comic Book Lettering since 2003. He has done lettering for many publishers, most notably and recently Avatar Press. He's also the only letterer working with Inception Strategies, an Aboriginal-Australian publisher that develops social comics with public service messages for the Australian government. Jaymes is also a 2012 and 2013 Shel Dorf Award Nominee.